M000240407

Girl With a Star Spangled Heart

Based on a True Story of Character and Courage

Elaine Fields Smith

Elaine Smith

Girl With a Star Spangled Heart

Girl With a Star Spangled Heart

Copyright 2015 Blazing Star Books

ALL RIGHTS RESERVED

Cover design by Cover Quintessa http://coverquintessa.blogspot.com

For information about this or other titles visit:

www.blazingstarbooks.com

ISBN: 978-0-9827690-8-9

First Edition

Chapter One

"Stand back everybody! Wilson RUN! Oh, no! It's gonna be a big one!"

Betty could hold in the sneeze no longer. She drew in a deep breath. "AAAHHHHCCCHHHOOOOO!" When recovered from being doubled over, she grabbed a small rock and threw it at her brother.

"Ouch! That hurt!" The straps of Nathan's patched overalls slipped onto his muscular shoulders as the teenager cranked with all his might. One stray curl fell over his forehead. Great effort was needed to bring up the long metal tube filled with water from the well. Betty grinned as the weight of the load in the cylinder almost lifted the teenager right off his feet.

She stood, manning a wooden bucket, awaiting the water. Neither she nor her younger sister Nancy cared one bit about getting their flour sack dresses dirty leaning on the rocks surrounding the well opening. Betty's little dog danced with excitement.

"Isn't he handsome?" The Boston Terrier's pointed ears perked up, as if knowing he was the focus of conversation. "I still can't believe Wilson is my dog." Betty knelt to scratch the little dog's chin.

Nancy put her hands on her hips. "Humph. It's downright amazing he's here at all, considering where he came from. The only reason that ugly John Henry Hannigen gave Wilson to you was to get you to go out with him. But even that shouldn't be enough." Nancy continued to watch for the cylinder. "That boy is ugly. Inside and outside."

Betty pictured John Henry. Tall. Lean, even downright skinny. Raggedy blonde hair he wore a bit too long. His smile was worse, the missing front tooth emphasized a rather mean streak. Wrinkling her nose, she sat on a rock.

"Now, Nancy. Be nice. Go out? Even if I wasn't frightened of the whole idea, Mama won't let me go out with *any* boy. Besides, I've heard a dog is better than a man any day. Ain't that right?"

She patted her leg for the dog to jump into her lap. "Yes it is, isn't it, sweetheart? Let me call you sweetheart, I'm in love with you..." Betty held her ear toward the dog's muzzle. He licked her neck and she laughed.

"Get up here!" Nancy grumbled, "And do your share!

"Ah, she's just plain jealous, ain't she, Wilson?"

"You're all wet, that's what you are!" Nancy grabbed the cylinder which had just emerged from the well. She released water directly on Betty's head. Wilson yelped, jumped away from the cold wetness and began barking. Betty hopped up from her perch on the rock.

"Oh, you're all wet! Look at you!" Nancy yelled about the dog's high pitched barking.

"Drat it! I worked hard to get that water!" Nathan seemed angry.

Betty studied his face, and knew right away he was just pretending to be mad.

"Did any go in the bucket?" Nathan asked.

Getting to her feet, Betty watched Wilson shake from head to his stubby little tail.

"I wish I could do that. Here," she said. "Let me wring out my dress over the bucket. Wouldn't want all that hard work to be wasted!"

She looked at Nancy. "My lands, little sister, you beat all." Betty dripped what water she could into the bucket. She then flung her sopping wet hair at Nancy, who dodged the spray and ran toward the house. Wilson chased after her for a bit, then circled around to come back to the well.

"I declare, that girl!" Betty told Nathan. "Send it back down in and I'll help pull it up this time." A breeze blew through the trees. "Ooh, that air is kind of cool!"

"It is October, in case you haven't noticed. A 'course it's cool!" Nathan pointed toward the cabin. "Go put on something dry." He winked." I'll bet you a biscuit at supper I can have the water drawn before you can get back!" He said, laughing.

"We shouldn't be bettin' but, you're on. I think Mama's making fried chicken for Sunday night supper," she said, walking backward. "That extra biscuit will go good with the gravy!" With that parting shot, Betty ran barefoot through the grass to the house.

The sturdy log cabin and barn with livestock and happy children belied an underlying poverty common to rural West Virginia in 1937. Every day, the Nugen family gave thanks for what they had, for starvation was not among the effects of The Great Depression. But while Robert Nugen's skill at farming and animal husbandry kept the family fed, there was no extra money, and cash or coin was a rare sight indeed.

3

Most everything the family needed came from their own fields and animals, or bartering those things for coal oil for lamps and buttons to replace those lost from the shirts and coats of twelve active children. Betty never went to bed hungry. But, at age seventeen, she was hungry for life.

She ached to experience the world beyond Fayetteville, West Virginia after graduating from high school. The more she learned about the land of ten thousand lakes in the state of Minnesota to the white, sandy beaches of Florida, the more she yearned for adventure. Magazines like *Time* and *National Geographic* at the school library took her on fanciful flights of imagination. She especially loved the photos of airplanes and admired the fashions of the day. The images excited the adventurer within the farm girl. But her inherent fear of the unknown kept that excitement in check. That, and Betty's loyalty, which ran deeper than her desires. The pretty, quiet girl loved her home and family without reservation. She adored her school, her state and the US of A.

Her clothes were old, but clean and neat. Dark brown curls crowned a beautiful face. Creamy skin covered a beautiful soul. Some of her vast capacity for love was given to the little dog, Wilson. Her father fussed that a Boston Terrier had no place on a farm. But when he petted the black fur, scratched the bat-like ears and admitted the animal wouldn't eat much, Betty knew Wilson could stay. He walked to school with her and waited patiently under a tree for her return trip home.

With twelve children in the family, nothing was truly owned by one person. Clothes were handed down, repaired and handed down again. The boys often used bits of rope to keep their oversized pants in place.

The fourteen year old Paul ran everywhere he went, bare feet carrying him from one adventure to the next. He was tall and thin, a born runner. Everyone had chores: Nathan fetched water,

Nancy fed the chickens, Paul fed the hogs, Betty milked the cow while Ethel cooked, washed and even cared for some of her nieces and nephews. Everyone helped when there were peas to shell or beans to snap. There was always work to do. Canning produce from the garden in summer, shucking corn and drying apples and making apple butter occurred later in the year. The older brothers and sisters had either married and begun their own families nearby or entered military service.

With an aptitude for arithmetic, Betty helped both Nancy and Paul with their schoolwork. Nancy was an avid reader, always coming home with books from the library which she often read aloud after supper by the light of a coal lamp.

The school and some stores in town had electricity, but the wires hadn't yet reached as far out as the Nugen farm. So while the children knew of such advances in the world as radio, telephone and motor cars, nothing like that existed in their home life. They found joy in simple everyday things, like rowdy games of tag or just sitting on the porch watching fireflies.

Unable to ignore her daughters' raucous entry the house, Ethel wiped her hands on her apron and turned away from her biscuit dough. "Great heavenly days, what are you girls up to now? Where's the water?"

"You're getting' *me* all wet!" Nancy shouted.

"That's what you get for getting' me all wet!"

The giggling diminished slightly at the sound of their mother's steps across the wooden floor. They called a truce and walked toward their mother.

"And where, pray tell, is the water I sent you to get?"

The sisters exchanged a quick look. Betty said, "Nathan's drawing more after little miss here wasted a whole bucket full on me," Betty grinned nervously. One never knew how Ethel might react to a bad situation.

"Wasn't wasted, it was worth it to see your face! Don't worry, mama, Nathan's drawing more. I'll help bring it up." Nancy wiped her wet arm on Ethel's apron.

"Stop that! You'll get me all wet. Well, Betty, you should take some soap to wash and set your hair since it's already wet. That nice Mr. Hannigen will be over this evening to take your photograph, remember?"

Nancy threw an elbow into Betty's side. "Oh yeah, our glamor girl is having a photo session."

Betty ignored her sister. "Oh, dear. I forgot all about it. Yes, I'll do that mama." She looked briefly at the floor. "Did...did Mr. Hannigen say anything about a dress? John Henry mentioned they had one. Oh I do hope he doesn't come along with his father. I am nervous enough about all this with him standin' around gawkin'." Betty asked.

"I don't know about John Henry, but yes, Mr. Hannigen is bringing his wife's old prom dress. "She caught Betty's eyes with a stern look. "This is your graduation picture, Betty Irene. We don't often get the chance to get photographs done. You'd best make it count. And if John Henry does come along, you *will* be nice to him."

"Yes, mama." Betty turned to find the soap and curlers for her hair. Nancy pretended to help, as their mother turned back to her dough and began kneading.

"Be nice to him?" Nancy whispered. "I hope it's worth trading your image on a photograph for..." She glanced at Wilson. "For a *dog*!"

Betty playfully back handed her sister's arm, then quickly pulled on a sweater and a pair of Paul's pants. She picked up her wet clothes, the box containing the brush rollers and motioned for Nancy to follow.

"Of course it's worth it!" Betty exclaimed when they were again outdoors. She hung her dress on the clothes line. As if on cue, the dog ran up to the girls and turned in an excited circle. "Because he's worth it!

Nancy stooped to pat the dog's head. She grabbed the hair brush and began smoothing Betty's wet curls.

"Do you believe the story...that Mr. Hannigen might send some of his photographs to that New Yorker magazine?" Betty sighed. "Wouldn't it be something if one of *me* was published?"

"Hummph. Personally, I think you'd hide under the bed if that happened."

Nancy had a point. If it happened, that is. "I'll cross that bridge when I come to it. The pictures are part of the deal for Wilson, so I'll just have to face it."

Nancy rolled her eyes, as Nathan approached, carrying the bucket of water. He poured a little into the wash bin the girls were using to rinse Betty's hair before walking on to the house. He stopped on the porch and called back, "You owe me a biscuit, missy."

Chapter Two

Ethel hummed a familiar tune, as she expertly cut through the joints and separated the parts of the chicken she had killed earlier in the day. Everything and everybody earned their keep on the farm. As soon as Nancy reported this particular hen had ceased to lay eggs, the chicken was destined for the frying pan.

The principal meat in the family's diet was pork thanks to the annual "Hog Killing Day" held each November. But supplies of pork were low in October, so a batch of fried chicken and chicken soup, if there were enough leftovers, would last a day or two.

The youngest of the Nugen children, Paul, sauntered into the kitchen and picked up a line of the song. "You get a line and I'll get a pole, honey. You get a line and I'll get a pole..." Another noise diverted his attention. "What's that?"

"Sounds like one of those motor cars. Oh! It is about time for Mr. Hannigen and his new-fangled camera." She turned to the open window. "You girls get in here!"

"A motor car! Oh, boy!" Paul jumped up from where he had been sitting and ran out the door.

Betty and Nancy also heard the racket, and looked toward the rocky path which led to the farm. Huge boulders, rooted deeply into the mountain, poked only the tops of their heads in the tire tracks making travel to the farmhouse a bumpy and sometimes precarious venture for a motor car.

The girls scooped up the cardboard box with the recently removed rollers and pins and hurried inside. Betty went first, appalled that a nonfamily member might see her in trousers. Wilson trotted happily behind.

"Goodness gracious, what will I wear till it's time to put on the dress? Thanks to somebody, my other dress is still wet!"

Ethel narrowed her eyes. "Never you mind about that. I'll handle Mr. Hannigan. Just wait out of sight."

The 1927 Model T sedan bounced over the last rocks before reaching the farm. It squeaked to a halt when a young Hereford steer with a halter and trailing lead rope blocked the way. Paul, running full speed toward the car, tried to grab the rope, and when that proved impossible, he jumped up and down, waving his arms.

"Git Beauregard! It's just a motor car. Don't be so nosy! You are such worry wart! You're always in the way! Now, GIT!" Paul slapped the steer on the rear to move him along and jogged beside the car as it rolled slowly toward the cabin.

"Mr. Hannigen, this is great! A real motor car! Will you give me a ride after while? I mean, if you have time…"

Ethel stepped onto the porch, still wearing her apron. "Now, Paul, don't bother Mr. Hannigen." She walked toward the car. "Betty is hoping you were able to bring a dress. Otherwise, this might not…"

"Never fear, ma'am. I've got it right here. That road of yours ain't much road." The man climbed out of the car backward and straightened his coat. He looked at the anxious boy peering in awe at the car. "If your mama says it's okay, you can ride down to the bottom of the hill with me and John Henry later. Though it might be a wee bit of a bumpy ride over them rocks."

"That road usually only sees the feet of animals and children. In fact, I do believe yours is only the second motor car to make it all the way up here!"

9

"Second?" The older man asked.

"No, mama, the third. Uncle D.L can make it and so can the doctor," Paul offered.

Mr. Hannigen reached through the open side of his car and brought out a pale pink pile of gauzy material. He handed it over to Ethel in an untidy bundle. He noticed the frown on her face. "Aw, now, don't look so worried. The wife says if you just hang it up for a few minutes, the wrinkles will fall out. You might need to fluff up the posy on the front, too. Somewhere in there is a matching hair bow, too. It will take me a bit to set up the camera and tripod." Turning a slow circle, he surveyed the terrain. Let's see, where's the best light and background?" He waved to his son. "Come on John Henry, boy, watch and learn. Ah, perhaps over here…"

Ethel grasped the dress close to keep its hem from dragging the ground. "Oh, are you teaching the boy that photography

"Yes, indeedy. He's gonna be a big time news photographer and take pictures like those of John Dillinger and all the people killed in that FDR assassination attempt a couple of years back." He gave a quick nod. "Glad they didn't get the old boy."

Paul perked up to enter the conversation. "Yeah, we learned in school about all those programs the president started, so's people could build things around the country. Guess them city people needed jobs."

Ethel turned toward the house. "I have biscuits in the oven. Paul, you help out however you can. And fetch them a drink of water."

The boy nodded understanding, and she made her way inside. She held the dress out at arm's length, eyeing the size. She

10

nodded once. Ethel woman knew nothing about photography, but had a lifetime of sewing experience. After a quick stop by the rocking chair to pick up her sewing basket, she disappeared into the side room with the dress.

Ten minutes later, Betty emerged from the cabin feeling like a princess. The pink layers of material floated as she walked. The bodice fit tightly, after Ethel employed several pins and whip stitches of thread to close up the gaps where the dress was too large. The skirt stretched out from the waist and down to the ground, covering the girl's bare feet. A crown of fabric flowers adorned her brown curls. But the princess was uneasy: John Henry had accompanied his father.

Hannigan smiled. "Ah, dear girl. You look lovely. Just lovely. Come over here by the trees and we'll take a couple of shots."

"Shots?"

"That's photographer's slang for taking the picture, brainless," John Henry said.

"That'll be enough of that, boy. Mind yourself. Let's get goin', the light is fading."

Mr. Hannigen positioned Betty in front of the tripod and disappeared under the camera's drape. His muffled voice could barely be heard. "Move to your left. No, that's not it. Sorry, I get confused under here. To your right. Yes, that's better. Ok, get ready and keep smiling..."

Betty did as she was told, wondering if it was possible for the camera to capture her fear and nervousness.

"All right, that's good. Now smile. That's right. Keep smilin'..."

11

Nancy, Ethel and Paul focused on the camera. Were they wondering, as Betty was, just what Mr. Hannigen was doing under the drape? She noticed Wilson's ears perk. Following the dog's line of vision, Beauregard the Hereford steer, emerged from the trees.

"I declare, Beau," she said, stroking the steer's head. "You beat all! Pickin' now, of all time, to get some attention!" Laughing, she looked at Paul. "Take him back to the barn, little brother. Before he snots all over this pretty dress!"

She heard a click, a whir, and Mr. Hannigen came out of hiding. Surely he hadn't taken a photograph of her petting the steer!

As Paul approached, Beauregard became interested in the photographer. He dodged the boy, and ran toward the tripod. Everyone—Paul, Nancy, Hannigen and even Ethel reached out to catch the camera. All but Ethel ended up on the ground in a tangle of arms and legs. Nancy saved the camera.

"Oh, my goodness," Betty whispered. "Oh, no... AAAHHHHCCCHHHOOOOO!"

"Lordy mercy. That sneeze could scare off a swarm of bees!"

Ethel glared at Hannigen. Her look was enough to keep him quiet. She turned her attention to the children.

"Git in the house and outta that dress, girl," Ethel scolded. "Nancy? You go on with her, help take out all them pins I stuck in it. Paul, you git that animal outta here, NOW!"

"Yes, mama," all three children said in unison.

Betty slowly walked toward the house, watching the frothy fabric swirl around her ankles. It reminded her of a mass of sunset drenched clouds.

From behind she heard a familiar huff-puff and turned. "Beauregard, go on now!" The steer was like a pet, ever since she'd been working with him for a 4-H project.

"Aw, Beau, you've really done it this time, you spoiled brat!" Paul grabbed the lead rope. "You best come with me, before Betty gets outta that fancy dress and whups you good." From the corner of her eye, Betty saw John Henry leaning on a tree with a smirk.

"C'mon! Or I promise, we'll we make ground meat outta you!" Paul led the steer away. "And you git, too! He pointed at John Henry. "I got a pretty good idea how ol Beau, here, got through the gate to mess up Betty's...shot."

Nancy, bless her heart, had plucked Betty's now-dry dress from the clothesline. She tossed it on the bed and hurried to remove the pins. "Mama's awful upset. I knew that boy was mean clear through. He spooked Beauregard on purpose. Why would he do such a thing while his pa's around?"

Betty sighed and shrugged, watching through the half open window as Mr. Hannigan loaded everything into his car, then stood beside the driver's door, blotting his forehead with a white handkerchief. With that cool breeze, why was he perspiring so?

"Nothing is broken, I hope," she heard her mother say. She knew by the way Ethel was standing she was not pleased.

"Oh, no, ma'am. It all looks fine. The extra plates were exposed, though, so no more picture taking today." He nodded toward Wilson, who sat protectively beside Ethel. Got one good shot, and if it develops up all right, it'll be a decent tradeoff for the dog."

He motioned to John Henry, who climbed into the passenger seat.

"I reckon we'll be on our way, then Mrs——."

"Hold on, there. What about the dress?" She faced the cabin. "Oh, here comes Nancy with it now." Facing Hannigen again, she said, "Well, I'm sure you're right. Whatever you got will be better than no photograph at all."

She took the dress from Nancy's outstretched arms. Ethel looked down at the beautiful fabric, and Betty saw her mother's fingers twitch slightly, as if she was fighting the temptation to wad the dress up into a ball, just as she had received it.

"As I always say, return something you borrowed in better shape than when you got it," she said handing it carefully to Hannigan. "How soon before we can see the picture?"

Hannigan tossed the dress into the back seat. "I'm not exactly sure. But when it's ready I'll bring a print out..."

Betty saw John Henry smirk, and evidently her mother did too. "That won't be necessary. My son, Nathan, can pick it up on his way home from work. He will stop by on Thursday, if that's agreeable."

The photographer climbed into his motor car. "I reckon I could have somethin' by Thursday," he said.

"Very well, then. Thank you and good day." Ethel turned and walked toward the cabin with Nancy close behind. Only when the three women stood inside the cabin, Nancy dared to speak.

"I've been wondering about something. How come we get Wilson *and* a photograph from Mr. Hannigen? What does he get out of it?"

Ethel harrumphed. "The way I understand it, they can make as many of those pictures as they want from that negative. You just keep a close eye on those magazines and such down at the library. If Betty's picture shows up in one of them, we'll know the answer to that question, 'cause Mr. Hannigen will get paid for every last one of 'em."

Nancy laughed "I'd sure be surprised anybody buy a picture of Betty and Beauregard!" Nancy exclaimed. Betty tried not to laugh, as their mother struggled to stifle a smile. The older woman quickly turned toward her work.

"We're gonna need more water, Ethel said, "To boil the chicken bones later." She exhaled a long sigh. "I sure hope your father gets the pump here at the house fixed soon."

"Yes, mama,' they said together. And as they raced across the yard, they heard her add, "And try not to spill it all over each other this time!"

Chapter Three

The family gathered on the porch after supper pretty often, especially during good weather. However, Ethel was known to sit in her rocker under the protection of the metal roof even during rain and snowfall. That old rocking chair got moved around more than any piece of furniture the Nugens owned. It was by the coal burning fireplace on winter evenings, by the window almost every day, on the porch after supper, and even out in the grass should Ethel want to sit in the sun.

She had given birth to twelve children and lived on a farm all her life. No wonder the woman felt older than her years. Though only in her mid-fifties, Ethel's body was tired. More specifically, her feet hurt. Therefore she sat in her rocker at every opportunity. But her spirit was strong and intellect sharp enough to regret her innate orneriness being passed down to some of her children.

Nancy in particular had a mischievous streak. Perhaps being the youngest girl contributed to her brashness. She played pranks on her siblings regularly, but not so consistently as to make them wary. After graduating from high school, Nathan went to work in the coal mine and brought home every penny of his pay to help the family. He had ideas of joining the Army, but his fondness for a certain girl in town kept him from wanting to leave home.

Paul rarely missed a day of school, and won the hearts of all who met him. A happy, sensitive boy, he was a joy to the entire family. And that was saying something, since the Nugen family was so big. On holidays, the older siblings and their families would converge on the farm, sometimes from as far away as Maryland.

Betty often thought about places beyond her home. Torn between the dreams of youth and the desire for stability and belonging, she faced her upcoming graduation from high school with trepidation. Not interested in any of the boys in Fayetteville, she, like many other young women of the time, sighed at photos of Clark Gable and John Wayne. Her blue eyes grew dreamy at the thought of Ginger Rogers dancing and the pin curls adorning lipsticked and rouged stars like Bette Davis and Myrna Loy.

Yet she also loved the feel of the cow's teat as it gave milk through her hands, the taste of green apples right off the tree and the fragrance of ripening peaches. She'd read about the dry air of the deserts of Arizona and the never sleeping New York City, but nothing could compare with the lush green hills of her beloved West Virginia.

Betty and her siblings almost always walked to school, often through freezing rain and snow. But they didn't mind. Bundled in layers of their older siblings' clothes, they walked, ran, and skipped down the dirt paths to town. The kids knew only the most affluent people in Fayetteville had motor cars and they were often unreliable in the muddy mess that the streets became after even a little moisture soaked into them. Horses and mules were commonly seen with riders and pulling small wagons.

Nathan rode the family mule to and from work on days Robert didn't need her to work the fields. Betty considered it a good possibility that the next summer, instead of Nathan, she would be riding that mule in a few months to a job in town. She sincerely hoped to make enough money to help her family. But a tiny spark of desire to get off the mountain still burned in her soul.

Living with so many siblings, Betty learned to do without. The boys had first choice of the pieces of fried chicken, so she learned to appreciate the more undesirable cuts. The two, small nodules of meat in the back were her favorites. The Nugen family was not picky; everyone ate what was presented and ate it

17

all. Only the prejudices of the parents' tastes limited the children from experiencing different foods. Ethel believed what they didn't know wouldn't hurt them. She especially disliked black eyed peas, just as her own mother had. Betty only knew of green peas, and therefore had no need for any other variety.

Sunday dinner was a usually busy affair. Fanny's three boys often returned home from church with their grandparents in the wagon. They romped about with Paul playing games and tormented the girls. When Fanny and D.L. appeared, the children took their plates onto the porch while the adults ate inside. After dinner, Fanny herded her brood back down the hill to their home not quite a mile down the road.

On one bright afternoon, Nathan picked up his harmonica or mouth harp as some called it, and began playing a song soft and low. Ethel and Betty hummed along while Nancy read from the book open in her lap. She looked into the distance as if thinking of something.

"Homework?" Ethel asked without looking up from her sewing. Nancy nodded and looked back at the book.

"Yes, ma'am. I have to memorize a poem." Nancy sighed. "It's odd how when you first read something like this you don't understand, but repeating it over and over, you can figure out what the writer was saying." She seemed to be studying the page in the book. Betty and Nathan fell silent.

"That's the way of the Bible, too, child," Ethel stated.

"Well, don't keep us in suspense, read the poem!" Betty said.

"I have to recite the whole thing. That's one reason I chose a short one. And that it made me think of something else. Here, you hold the book and check me on it." Nancy stood on the edge of the porch facing the family. Paul began to giggle, but Nathan kicked him to be quiet. With a deep breath, she began softly.

"If I Had But Two Little Wings, by Samuel Taylor Coleridge (1772-1834)

If I had but two little wings
And were a little feathery bird,
To you I'd fly, my dear!
But thoughts like these are idle things
And I stay here.

But in my sleep to you I fly:
I'm always with you in my sleep!
The world is all one's own.
And then one wakes, and where am I?
All, all alone.

"My word, that sounds awfully sad, doesn't it?" Ethel asked.

"Mama, poetry usually is sad, or full of lots of sappy love." Betty answered. "This one sounds like both." She handed the book back to her sister.

"There, you see? You don't understand it the same as me. I can picture the National Geographic and other magazines with pictures of faraway places and strange looking people. You see? We can experience those things through the photographs, but we are still here."

"Yes, that's true," Betty agreed. "But it couldn't be as good as actually being there. Plus, I believe it would take more than two little wings to get you off this mountain!"

"More like the wings of an airplane," Nathan offered. As if on cue, two small aircraft flew directly over the house. He ran with the others into the yard to watch.

19

"Isn't it amazing how they just stay up there like that?" Nancy asked, as she peered into the sky.

"Not really amazing, just mathematics. Velocity and lift coefficients combined with some rigid structure means you can fly" Betty offered. The engines droned on, even as the planes faded from sight. "What's amazing is that they're probably going over a hundred miles an hour. Imagine! They could be going to Washington D.C."

Nathan and Nancy looked at their sister with surprise. Betty shaded her eyes in effort to watch the airplanes as long as possible. She sighed deeply, and then was startled when she realized they were staring. "What? Oh, you all go on."

"Maybe it's Betty what wants some wings!" Paul teased. Betty grabbed at his shirt and they all walked back to the covered porch. Two old barrels with attached lids stayed permanently on the end of the porch near the water well. One was used to catch rainwater from the metal roof and both often served as perches for the children when all the chairs were taken. Betty hopped up on one while Wilson jumped on a large log and then onto the lid of the second barrel. The girl and dog often spent hours in that position while she read or sewed and with him keeping watch.

Sunday was a day of rest except for the essential tasks which had to be done each and every day. Betty and the others did their chores after church and before lunch. One reason was to avoid the rowdy McKinney boys for a while; another was to get everything done so they could do their school work later in the afternoon. Betty opened the book she left there earlier in the day and noticed her father near the barn. He was moving slower than usual and leaning on a shovel. The sight reminded her of something.

"I remember part of a poem I studied last year." Betty said thoughtfully. "It's by Edwin Markham. Let's see...it goes like this:

Bowed by the weight of centuries he leans
Upon his hoe and gazes on the ground,
The emptiness of ages in his face
And on his back the burden of the world.

"It's kinda sad," Betty concluded.

"Poppa must be hurting," Paul said. "I'll go help him."

"No, son. Leave him be. He wouldn't take your help anyway. Proud, that man," Ethel said severely before turning back to her needle. "Betty Irene, your studies are going all right?"

"Yes, mama. Just fine. I'll have no problem grad..."

"Look out, here it comes!" Nancy cried.

"AAAHHHHCCCHHHOOOOO!"

"Bless you," Ethel grinned. "Poor child, you sneeze just like your grandma. She had the hay fever, too. Well, at least you'll be very blessed..."

Wide eyes all around met the unexpected joke from Ethel. Then they all broke out in laughter before dispersing around the home to their own interests.

Later in the afternoon, the atmosphere around the house was melancholy, as everything quieted down and Robert was obviously not feeling well. Limping from the barn to the house, he sat on a step with his leg stretched out. He rubbed the muscles, wincing with pain. At age sixty, the long hours, hard work of running a farm, and the duties toward a wife and twelve children had taken its toll.

21

His knees were worn out and ulcerative varicose veins caused terrible itching, pain, and sometimes bleeding in one of his legs. Betty often helped him straighten it out on the bed and Ethel would place a cloth soaked in freshly drawn, cold water from the well over the affected area. The coolness and pressure eased the discomfort to the point he often drifted off to sleep.

The children were somewhat afraid of their father. He was old, distant and gruff, uneducated yet very capable of running the family farm. Insistent that his children get an education, each of the boys had completed at least ten years of school. Betty was the first girl to make it to grade twelve. Here older sisters were married and doing all right. Both Ethel and Robert wanted Betty and Nancy to get their high school diplomas. Robert didn't see the importance to actually finish school, but agreed it would do no harm. With his wife slowing down, the girls were a lot of help with Paul and the grandchildren down the hill. Nancy approached him from the rear.

"Papa? We learned in school about a thing that wraps around tightly and puts pressure on places that hurt. It's supposed to ease the pain. I was thinking we could try wrapping some strips of fabric around that place on your leg. If you want to try it." She backed up a step as Robert turned toward her.

"Silly new fangled ideas. Don't fuss over me, girl. Nathan, you and the boy fetch water for the barrels this week. We'll be killin' the hogs Saturday when everybody's here to help. The pigs is ready and I feel cold weather coming in my bursitis. It's time." He rose and limped away.

"Pride. It'll kill him some day, it will," Ethel shook her head side to side. She watched her husband of almost forty years walk slowly back to the barn before returning to the sewing on her lap.

22

Betty had been through many a Hog killing day. It was a tremendous event on the family farm. Usually four to five pigs were slaughtered and processed to hang in the smokehouse all winter. Pork was a principal source of meat for the Nugens, so great care was taken to utilize every part of the animal.

A large A-frame structure used each year was reassembled and patched with scrap wood and nails, the pulley and rope attached, and the entire configuration erected near the front porch. Earlier in the week, Ethel and the girls moved the barrels onto short metal stands near the A-frame before Nathan and Paul began filling them with water.

Wilson made every step with Betty, as she fetched and arranged the wood below the barrels. The fire was set under each, and Ethel's rocking chair sat close by so she could direct the activities. Everyone had an assignment, whether it was pulling on the rope to raise the carcass into the air, deliver the pig parts to the barrels to be scalded and skinned, or catch the blood and organs for separate processing. Even the McKinney boys were enlisted to keep the fires blazing.

With everyone's attention elsewhere, Betty's dog was uneasy. The smell of blood and fresh meat further agitated little Wilson. Betty was occupied with handing the cut parts of the pig and placing them in the boiling water in the very same barrel she usually sat on. Sitting down by Ethel's chair, he watched Betty walk toward the barrel with a pig's foot. He hopped up on the rocking chair and jumped upward, toward the top of the barrel.

"Oh, NOOOOO!!!" Betty screamed in horror as Wilson fell into the boiling water. Everyone turned to see what was happening. One glance into the barrel sent Betty running away, sobbing and clutching her sides. Bloody from handling the meat, she fell to the ground still screaming. "Oh, no, no, no, NO!"

23

"Stand back!" Nathan quickly grabbed the large tongs used to pull the scalded meat from the boiling water and took hold of the dead dog, lifting him out of the barrel. Nancy turned away. Paul ran to his mother who clutched him tightly. Nathan laid Wilson on the porch and looked at his father for instructions.

"Go to her. We will keep on here, after…" Robert said. He sadly looked at the little dog. "Paul, we'd best bury him right away before she…. Come on boy."

Paul pulled away from Ethel, sniffing back tears. Nathan hurried to Betty where she was crouched in the grass. The old man gently picked up the dog and Paul followed him toward the barn.

Betty and Nathan had a special bond and feeling for each other. He put a hand on her back. Feeling the sobs and heaving breathing, he pulled her into an embrace. The pig's blood on her hands and face was streaked with hot tears. He rocked her back and forth gently. After a few minutes she regained control and pulled back to look at her brother. "He's dead, isn't he?" A fresh tear pushed out of her eye.

Nodding, Nathan grasped her hand and pulled her up.

"Oh, poor puppy. I feel so…responsible," she whispered. Standing, he hugged her again.

"Not your fault, sis. Not anyone's fault. It was just an accident. He didn't know…" She nodded understanding and they walked back to the house. Ethel instructed them to go to the well and wash off with fresh water before returning to the work. Betty grasped her gentle brother's hand, as they slowly walked toward the well.

Chapter Four

Betty's last year winter in school was cold and hard. She and Nancy used a coal oil lamp for light and what little heat they gave off in the girl's room. Betty missed Nathan, who was staying in town. Paul was allowed to sleep in the loft above the girls' room. Ethel saw to it the fires in the wood stove and small fireplace were kept going night and day. No one in the cabin noticed the wood smoke. Only when the girls were at school did they realize their hair and clothing smelled smoky. But most everyone else smelled much the same, so it wasn't really a problem.

The spring of 1938 promised many things to the Nugens, especially Betty. Snow melted revealing rich earth ready to receive seed. The milk cow had given birth to a fine Jersey heifer. Nancy planned to raise her and show the animal at the county fair in the fall. Life around the farm was moving forward and Betty became more and more anxious about leaving school. With no marriage prospects, and none desired, she stopped at the Hammer Five and Dime in Fayetteville regularly to appear to shop and ask quietly about a job. She had good grades in school, a letter of recommendation from one of her teachers. These and her dependable reputation served as a resume.

Graduation should have been a grand event for Betty. But, as a rule, no parents could afford the pomp and circumstance trappings of a ceremony, so diplomas were presented to the twelve graduates on the last day of school in June. With that piece of paper in hand, she again visited the Hammer's store. Impressed with her, Henry Hammer hired her on the spot. On that day, she walked out with a job—a rare and precious occurrence at the peak of The Depression.

In preparation for being out of school, Betty and her mother made skirts from every piece of fabric big enough for the pattern.

Her one white blouse would have to serve until she could afford to get more clothes. She would wear boots while walking to work, then change into her mother's Sunday shoes.

As Betty's meager pay came in, she gave everything directly to Ethel. Spring had been exceptionally dry and the crops were not growing as well as they should. Chores continued, less chickens were kept, but more butter was churned with the extra milk from the mama cow, as Betty could easily sell the fresh butter in town. Spending the summer days inside the store was agony for the young woman. She longed for the outdoors and running barefoot in the grass around the cabin. Nancy and she were still close, often whispering in the darkness after bedtime.

The Five and Dime was much like a general store, with many dry goods and some canned food. Betty stocked the shelves and took care of customers. Her proficiency with addition and subtraction served very well in tallying bills and making change. She marveled at the currency, not ever seeing much folding money in her life. Counting the till at closing time was a particular delight. The feel of the money in her hands was almost intoxicating. But no thought of theft or other immoral action ever occurred to Betty Nugen. She was raised to be honest and hardworking, and that's what she gave to the Five and Dime.

In October, Betty was excused from Hog Killing Day on the farm. She worked on Saturday and due to the unhappy circumstance the year before she was glad to stay away. She heartily missed Wilson through that cold winter. But where he would have stayed during the long days she was gone, she didn't know. Who knows? He might have been good company for Ethel. But Betty still wished for his presence.

When Halloween rolled around, people dressed up like cowboys or gypsies and there were many small ghosts in sheets during the costume parade. Betty never cared for scary costumes, so she went to work that October 31st with a bit of dread. When she got to the store, several people were clustered around the front door. They seemed quite upset, with arms waving about and yelling at each other. One man was waving a newspaper.

"It was just a radio show, its right here in the paper."

"I heard it, I tell ya. It was real!" One man exclaimed.

"The reporter said machines were wading across the Hudson into New York City. Why would they make that up?"

Another added. "They said 'We interrupt this program for a special bulletin.' That means there was a special bulletin for something that was actually happening!"

Betty hesitantly approached the men, as they were between her and the door, plus she was self-conscious of her muddy boots. A few sheets of the Monday morning edition of the Charleston Gazette dropped from one of the men's hands. The front page landed at Betty's feet and she quickly read the headline of the story they were discussing.

"Radio 'Hallowe'en' Play Causes Mass Hysteria in Nation," she read aloud. But directly across the page, another headline "New War Monster," and "Nazi Crowd Demonstrate Against Jews. Milling Mobs Threaten Revenge for Beatings of Germans Abroad 'By Vermin.' Parley Begins Today on Mass Expulsion – 10,000 Hebrews Returned From Polish Border Await Decision." She reached down and picked up the paper. The men then noticed the pretty girl behind them.

"Oh, excuse me, Miss Betty, are we in your way?" One of the men who knew her from church said.

"No sir, but...may I keep this part of the paper?" Betty presented the front page.

27

"Here, missy. Have the whole thing. I've got a car load of 'em, was just delivering the Gazette to this backwater town. It was a fake, men. There are no Martians in New York...California, maybe..." The newspaper deliveryman gave Betty the paper and walked quickly away.

She hurriedly scanned the story titled "Hysteria" and looked nervously at the remaining men. Coming to a quick decision, Betty called up her nerve to speak out loud.

"Martians? There is no such thing. I do believe those radio people played a mighty fine hoax on their listeners," she remarked. "What's much more important is this story on the other side of the page about what's going on in Germany. It says here mobs smashed windows all over the Jewish part of Berlin and arrested hundreds of people. No doubt innocent people, minding their own business. The more I hear about those Nazis, the more I fear another war."

"Yeah, if England could muster enough gumption to blow 'em off the face of the earth, we'd have nothing to worry about. You, of all people, Miss Betty, shouldn't be concerned about what's happening on the other side of the world. A pretty thing like you shouldn't have anything to do with that stuff. My brother was in France in The Great War, and he said there's nothing left in Europe to save, anyway."

Betty looked at the man with disbelief. "There are people there, Mr. Prater. Our ancestors lived there. Times are different now from twenty years ago, sir. Superior weapons, tanks, and airplanes are at our disposal. We, the USA, might have to do something."

The men were taken aback at the fervent tone and knowledge of the young woman. She turned and walked proudly into the store with the newspaper. Mr. Prater raised an eyebrow while the other shrugged his shoulders before continuing their walk around the town square.

Fall moved into winter and Betty continued her job at the Five and Dime, cashing her pay voucher at the bank and taking all but a few quarters to Ethel. Robert's legs were getting worse, the crops from the summer before had yielded less than ever before without his close attendance and care. But with Nathan and Betty's income, the family survived. One day in early spring, Nathan and Betty walked up the road toward their home.

"I've decided, sis. Our older brothers went in and did all right. Besides, I read they're gonna make a law to draft us anyway. This way I can get in whatever outfit I want. Plus, it'll be good to see other places and such," he said softly.

Betty held his hand. "But, but, there could be war soon. Is the mine so bad?" She asked.

"I'll die a young man if I stay down in that coal mine. I can feel the dust in my lungs. It's the darkness down there and the smell…it's bad. Yeah, it's that bad."

Betty squeezed his hand and released it. "With papa selling off some of the land, I don't know how we'll make it. Paul shouldn't be a farmer-he's too smart. I can't be a farmer…or even a farmer's wife, apparently." Betty sighed. It was well known she had no marriage prospects. She was practically an old maid at twenty-one. "Yes, I can see going into the military is right for you, Nathan. See the world, send us money, and try to stay alive."

"You can count on that! Don't you worry about not having a husband, sis. There ain't nobody around here good enough for you, and that's a fact. Besides, I bet something will happen that will get you off this mountain, too."

"I don't necessarily want to get off this mountain! It's my home and I love everything here. It's just that I...oh, dear...AAHHHCCCHHHOO!" While she was bent over from sneezing, she picked up a rock. "I might..." Rearing back, she threw the rock as hard as she could at a tree trunk beside the road. It struck with a "crack" and bark chips sprayed from the impact zone. She turned to her brother who stood with his mouth hanging open in surprise. "It's just that I might have to."

Chapter Five

Betty often helped Mabel Hammer, the store owner's wife and bookkeeper. With her skill with arithmetic, great memory, and strong work ethic, Betty was a valued employee. The two women often looked over the Charleston Gazette over a cup of tea in the morning. Betty read aloud a news article from the AP wire about the New York World's Fair to open in April 1939.

"Can you imagine? What a sight!" Mabel slapped her hand on the table. "This says they transplanted 10,000 trees and over a million tulip bulbs. A million! And there's a quarter million pansies along forty miles of pathway. My word, no wonder you need busses and trains to get around," Mabel cried.

"That would surely be something to see, wouldn't it?" Betty looked back at the paper. "And it says there's a huge building that's real modern looking."

"Yes, right here it says there's a huge sphere, I guess they mean round like a ball, that's connected to another building by a long moving sidewalk they call a 'helicline.' How odd. Here, look at the photo."

Betty peered at the black and white photograph of what appeared to be a large, white ball with a diagonal flat surface filled with people standing about which seemed to disappear into the side of the ball. She glanced again at the copy in the article and noticed a statement.

"Listen to this. The reporter says, 'The idea back of it all, folks, is demonstration of a happier way of American living through a recognition of the interdependence of man, and the building of a better world of tomorrow with the tools of today.' That sounds really interesting, though I'd never be able to go to something like that."

31

"Me, either, girl. New York's a long way from Fayetteville. Oh well. The newspaper will probably have lots of pictures. But seeing all those multicolored tulips and pansies in bloom would be simply breathtaking." Mabel folded the paper. "Make us another cup of tea, please dear, and we'd best get to work." Betty took their cups to the small kitchen in the back of the store.

As she lit a match to ignite the natural gas burner on the small stove, Betty thought about the way water and gas was brought into the kitchen. Turning the knob caused water to come out of the faucet spout. No pumping of a handle and certainly not drawing it from a well. Turning the handle on the burner caused a foul smelling gas to be distributed in a circular pattern. The store also had gas lighting which was used most often on the shorter, grey days in winter. The Nugens had only wood and coal fires for cooking and heat as well as candles and oil lamps for lighting. Betty was truly amazed at the ease in which the task could be done in town. And, for a moment, considered what life might be like off the mountain.

Betty's thoughts were interrupted by an argument in the office. She hesitantly entered, not wishing to intrude, before Mabel motioned her to come in. With the cup of tea delivered, she stepped backward and turned to leave.

"Just a moment, dear, don't leave. Betty and I were just having the conversation about things of the future, weren't we? If motion pictures can be shown and heard on a screen in a building, and radio can be broadcast all over the U S of A, why couldn't a signal of some sort carrying moving pictures and sound be sent from one place and received in another?"

"Silly, expensive pipe dreams…" Henry said before leaving the room. Betty was glad her employers weren't arguing in front of her.

"Well, I guess that's a sore subject," Mabel snickered while stirring her tea.

"What is?" Betty asked with a glance over her shoulder to be sure her boss was gone.

"Why, television, dear. As soon as electricity gets to this side of Fayetteville, I am proposing we put in a line of televisions. He's dead set against it. But the folks used to having radio will eat up television. Imagine seeing the faces of Dick Tracy or The Lone Ranger and Tonto. The cars and the horses and the variety shows. It will really be something if it works. Oh well, that's years away. All right, dear, let's get to that inventory list."

Betty fell into a routine at the store and at home with work of all types taking much of her time. She missed Nancy. After she graduated from school in 1939, Nancy learned to drive and moved in with their older sister who ran a taxi business in Oak Hill, ten miles from Fayetteville.

After Nathan shipped off to the Army, Betty looked forward to his postcards and he faithfully sent money home to his mother. Work around the farm fell mostly to Paul, but Betty also performed many difficult chores. She slept on the same feather mattress as she had from an early age.

While in the bank, Betty heard people say Franklin Delano Roosevelt appeared to be headed for a third term as President of the United States. Everyone knew the success of the projects he implemented in effort to pull the country out of the depths of the Depression. The papers reported manufacturing numbers were on the rise; arms, aircraft and vehicles of all types were being shipped to England for use in the defense of their country and holdings in the war with Germany. Millions of young men were employed by the government in programs such as the Works Progress Administration or Civil Conservation Corps. However, poverty ran rampant through the farming communities of America.

With electricity installed in only half of Fayetteville, Betty was glad Mac's Diner was on the right side of town. The bright, electric lights and radio on the counter made Mac's the center of attention, when the signal came in clearly from Charleston, the capital of West Virginia. Sometimes it wasn't so clear, but often it worked fine. Most popular with the locals were the fifteen minute segments of music played during the dinner hour-"The Dance Orchestra" and "Dinner Dance."

Betty often walked past the diner just to hear the music playing before riding back out to the country with Fanny's husband who had acquired an old Ford to drive to and from the mine. It was better than walking. Betty noticed the sounds of orchestras playing swing music were very different from the church hymns and folk songs she heard growing up. The fact that those radio programs played recorded music and transmitted it through the air to an electrical device in a Fayetteville diner was almost unbelievable. But the evidence was right there in on the counter. Men and women gathered around the radio and some even danced. Betty never went in, however. A cup of coffee cost money she didn't have. All her pay went directly to Ethel to help keep the family going.

When one of the older sisters became too large for some of her clothing after having a baby, she gave three dresses to Betty. She and Ethel altered them enough to fit nicely and she rotated days wearing them. Betty also had the few cotton skirts and two white blouses to alternate outfits between the dresses. Never in her life had she had such a wardrobe nor the need to actually have space to hang her clothes. After suffering the embarrassment of wearing muddy shoes in town, she took to wrapping scrap fabric around them to walk down the hill to ride with Fanny's husband into town. The rags stayed in the floor of the car during the day and she retrieved them for her walk back up the hill. When she was at work or walking around town, Betty appeared as neat as possible.

Ethel waited anxiously each day for Betty to bring the mail up the hill. Often letters from her sons in the service would arrive. She read them over multiple times and allowed Betty to read them, too. According to the papers, the radio and the letters, a threat of war hung over the entire nation. Nathan wrote of rifles which could fire multiple rounds very quickly and armored tanks with very large caliber cannon. He described Navy battleships bristling with machine guns and Army aircraft with gun barrels built into the wings.

Betty was fascinated by the fact bullets fired from those guns were perfectly timed to pass through the rapidly rotating engine propeller. The calculations involved were intriguing to the farm girl. Not looking forward to her twenty-second birthday, often wondered what she was going to do. What she *should* do.

She realized the country was evolving and taking great strides and leaving the folk of Fayetteville behind. But the coal had to be mined and pigs slaughtered. Soap was made as well as preserves and dried apples. But the crops in the Nugen field grew sparse as Robert had more and more trouble with his legs.

Betty learned to cook on the wood stove, excelling in baking yeast rolls and biscuits. A biscuit with a bit of ham or chicken had served as lunch since she had been a school girl, and Betty never tired of the sandwich. A thinly spread layer of freshly churned butter added some flavor and moisture to the biscuit and she carried a shaker of salt to spice up half of a turnip or potato she often had to eat with the small sandwich.

Occasionally a young man who worked at the bank across the square came into the Five and Dime. He sometimes bought shoe strings, other times just browsed the stationary section. Furtive glances toward the young woman stocking the shelves with candles and matches were noticed by Mabel, but not by Betty. On April 1, 1940, he stepped up to the counter with a notepad to purchase.

After Betty wrote out the receipt, the man asked to borrow her pen. He opened the notebook and wrote out a short message, tore it from the pad, and pushed it face down across the counter toward the panic stricken Betty. He quickly left the store. Mabel hurried to the sales counter.

"Well, dear. Are you going to read it?" She asked with fingers twitching to pick up the note.

"Oh my. He scared me half to death." Betty's hand shook. She pushed the note toward Mabel. "You read it, please."

Mabel read the note with a knowing smile. "My dear Betty, you have a date. He wants to take you to a movie in Oak Hill Saturday night at 7:00. Even gave you a choice; "Gone With the Wind" or "Clouds over Europe."

"A movie?" Betty was horrified. "With a man?"

"Of course with a man, honey. He's asked you out on a date!"

"I've never, well, yes. I've never been on a date and I don't know how!" Betty seemed close to tears.

"Deary, dear. It is no big thing. Going to the movies. You've been to the movies?"

"Only once or twice and that was with Nancy and Nathan. Okay, okay, let me think a minute. Let me see that note," Betty had regained her composure. "Well, I've read about "Clouds Over Europe. It's a spy movie with airplanes and Laurence Olivier. I'd, I think I'd like to see that one."

"You're twenty-two years old. It's high time for you to go to the movies on a date, my dear girl. And you want spies and airplanes when you could see one of the great love stories of our time and Clark Gable." Mabel sighed. "Well, it's up to you. If you want to go, write out your acceptance and I'll deliver it when I take over the day's deposits." Mabel walked away to leave her employee alone to write the note.

However, Betty left the sales counter empty handed and went back to work stocking the shelves. About an hour later she walked to the counter and picked up the pen. After looking at the ceiling for a while, she put down the pen down and walked away.

"What am I going to do with that girl?" Mabel asked herself aloud before walking out into the store. "I'm going to the bank in a few minutes, Betty," she said loudly. Betty sighed and walked behind the counter. By the time Mabel arrived at the cash register, Betty had written and folded the note.

"You're right, Mabel. I guess I should go." Betty's hands shook nervously. "But what will he think of me wanting to see the airplane movie? Oh, it doesn't matter, that's what I want. Can I get ready after work at your house and he...he pick me up there? As you know, no modern motor car can make it up our hill."

"Certainly dear. And I'll loan you some nice shoes and earrings. Don't worry." Mabel put an arm around Betty, seeing her discomfort. "You'll be fine. He's a nice boy. Well, he is the banker's son. When I get back we'll pick out some lipstick for you."

37

"Wait a minute, will you? I know! I'll write a quick letter to Nancy and have her meet me at the theater so I'm not all alone. Would you mail it for me?"

"Of course! Good idea. Always have a Plan B, I say." Mabel patted Betty's hand and left her to write the letter.

After the Five and Dime closed on Saturday afternoon at five o'clock, the two women walked to Mabel's home. Betty changed clothes, tried on shoes and received attention to her appearance like never before. Mabel set Betty's hair, applied makeup and clipped shiny earrings onto her earlobes. When Betty looked in the mirror, she almost didn't recognize herself. A young woman looked back with shock on her face and fear in her eyes.

"Beautiful, my dear. You'll be fighting off the men when you come out of that shell." Mabel took Betty's hand. "Not quite a princess, but certainly too good for *that* banker's son. But it's a step in the right direction, dear. You can't stay a clerk at the Five and Dime forever."

Betty felt even more fear, before Mabel held her in a hug like she had never known before. The woman's arms gave Betty strength and she felt more confident. When Mabel held her out at arm's length, Betty smiled.

"Thank you, Mabel. You're a good friend...and boss!"

When the motor car rolled to a stop in front of the house, Betty tried to calm her nerves and keep from throwing up. Almost before she knew it, she was swept from the front porch, into the car, and was riding down the dirt streets of Fayetteville with a man she didn't know. His smile was pleasant enough, but the noise of the engine prohibited any conversation. With only a windshield and no side glass, wind whipped at Betty's hair and the collar of her blouse.

She gripped the door for support with one hand, while the other attempted to keep her hair and blouse in place. The windy fifteen minute trip to Oak Hill seemed to take forever. Betty desperately hoped Nancy got the letter in time to know to rescue her from enduring a return trip in the open car. Surely she could bring one of the taxi cars!

Arriving at the theater, Betty waited, as she had been coached, to allow her date to rush around the car to help her out. One of Mabel's shoes fell off, as she stepped out of the vehicle. Embarrassed, she hurriedly shoved her bare foot back into it. Other, fashionably dressed women were walking arm in arm with their men into the theater. Some wore nylons and others sported hats with feathers and netting. Across the parking lot, Betty saw her sister, Alice's taxi cab. With a sigh of relief, she knew Nancy was close by. She felt her elbow grasped by the young man's hand, as they walked into the theater.

Flashing a five dollar bill, he paid for two tickets and made a show of placing the ones he received in change back into the wallet seemingly filled with money. Betty noticed his sly grin as he directed her to the concession counter. It was there Betty made eye contact with Nancy. She could see the almost frightened look on Betty's face and the smug smile of the banker's son as he slid an arm around her waist. When Betty felt his hand on her back, she jumped and moved away. The message was delivered. Nancy moved toward the couple.

"Well, sister dear! Fancy meeting you here!" Nancy embraced Betty to move her out of the man's reach. "It's been ages since I've seen you."

"Nancy! What a...a surprise! You haven't up the hill in over a month. Mother misses you. And me, too! Are you here alone?"

"Tonight, yes. My latest love interest is out of town. A girl's got to find something to do." She looked around Betty at the man. "Are you buying the popcorn? Isn't that nice?"

The banker's son had no choice but to purchase three sacks of popcorn and three cups of soda. The trio moved into the theater and took their seats. When the lights went down to show the newsreels, images of a bomb ravaged London appeared showing the devastating damage from German aircraft bombers. Betty was transfixed. The sight of the massive air fields with both English and American planes taking off and landing excited her.

Leaning toward Nancy, she whispered, "Imagine, our brothers might be there!"

Nancy shushed her sister and they continued to watchmen in uniforms with goggles on their heads and mechanics with rolled up sleeves crawling all over a large airplane. The film included still photos of smoke-filled streets and civilians huddled in a dark subway tunnel. Just as a vivid photo of the front of a brick building bursting outward from an explosion of a bomb within its walls appeared, Betty felt something on her knee.

Out of instinct, she swung a backhand to remove the intruding annoyance. Instead, her hand was grasped by the banker's son a bit too firmly. With a strong pull, Betty withdrew her hand and placed it in her lap. Eyes glued to the screen, more images of the war in Europe created an emotional reaction in the crowd, including Betty. The sight of a cathedral dome, bathed in light and intact among the smoking ruins of the surrounding area seemed jubilant. Then a still photograph of three children sitting on the rubble of what was the home the day before caused some people to shed tears and others to shout with anger. Betty reached across to touch her sister's arm and leaned in close to whisper.

"In a while let's go to the powder room. This just doesn't feel…right."

Nancy nodded and gripped her sister's hand. The movie began and they settle in to watch. An exciting tale unfolded of spies and a dashing Laurence Olivier as the brave pilot. Betty was riveted by the plot and equipment shown to be used in England. At one point in the movie, she shifted in the seat and found the banker's son leaning toward her.

"Watch in the upper right hand corner of the screen. Watch for a black dot," he whispered in her ear.

Betty pulled away and again paid close attention to the film. She noticed the women's dresses were hemmed just below the knee. Her skirts were much longer, almost down to her ankles. With a furrowed brow, she felt an arm on hers.

"Look, there it is, there's the warning dot," he said.

Nodding Betty acknowledged she did see the black dot in the corner of the screen. The banker's son grasped her arm and pulled her closer.

"That's the signal for the projector room to change reels. When the first dot comes up, they get ready, and when the bigger dot shows, they change reels to keep the film going without a break."

Betty glanced in the young man's direction and nodded again in understanding. Then she pulled his hand from her arm and leaned back toward Nancy. Suddenly a dramatic scene in the movie grabbed her attention and she again became captivated. She couldn't help but watch for the black dots in the corner of the screen. In the darkness of the theater, she failed to notice the banker's son stretching his arm overhead and down behind her shoulders. When his hand rested on her shoulder, she reacted automatically by throwing an elbow into his side. He quickly withdrew the arm and cradled his ribs.

"I'm sorry," Betty whispered. "I have older brothers. Learned to protect myself..." She pulled away and locked elbows with Nancy. At that moment, the black dots flashed, the film stopped, and the lights came on indicating an intermission. Quickly turning to her date she said, "We're going to the powder room. Be right back." The two women followed a wave of women hurrying to the ladies' room.

Several women "freshened" their makeup and hovered around the mirror for quite some time. When the two sisters were alone, Nancy pulled Betty into the corner.

"What's the matter with you? You're acting like a scared rabbit! He has to be the best catch around Fayetteville. His family has money, for goodness sake!"

"I don't know. It is just...wrong. Didn't you notice he was trying to touch my leg and my...side."

"Well, I'll admit that's not very gentlemanly since you two haven't even spoken much. But, do you want to be an old maid?"

"Better that than being tied to someone I don't care for," Betty looked in the mirror and smoothed her hair.

"How do you know you don't like him?"

Betty turned to her sister. "When his hand was on my arm, I swear it burned like he was the devil or some horrible thing. And there's something about the look in his eyes that...well, it scares me."

Nancy considered for a moment. "All right, so he gives us the creeps. I saw that devilish glint, too. But that's not all of it. What are you afraid of?"

"Afraid of?" Betty took a deep breath. "I guess I'm afraid of life, Nancy. And war. And I'm afraid if I got attached to someone he'd be drafted and disappear. If we get in the war, every able bodied man will have to go. My life is here, at home. Papa's health is failing and mama needs me. Even Paul will be gone soon."

"But you are entitled to your own life, dear. Oh, drat, you're right this guy isn't "the one." Well, do you want to see the rest of the movie, or bug out right now?"

"We have to stay until the end to not be completely impolite. But I don't have to sit next to him. And I'm not going to." The lights in the ladies room flickered indicating intermission was almost over. "Besides, I want to find out what happens…in the movie. Come on."

"Wait a minute. There's something on my mind. I need a piece of paper. We'll stop at the soda counter."

Betty watched as Nancy jotted down some lines of a poem she learned in high school, altering it a bit for her own purpose. Slipping it in her purse, she took Betty's arm and they reentered the theater. The bankers' son was relieved to see his date hadn't run away as he feared, but was chagrined when she left an open seat between them and placed her jacket on it. Nancy's coat was also placed on the seat, giving the definite signal it was not to be occupied.

When two more sets of flashing dots in the corner of the screen had passed, and at last Lawrence Olivier had solved the mystery and kissed the heroine, the lights came up. Nancy stepped across Betty to get her coat and face the banker's son.

"Thank you for bring my sister to Oak Hill. She's going to stay over with me. This is for you and now you just run on back home." She handed the slip of paper to the astonished young man and the two women rushed from the theater.

When they were safely tucked in the taxi cab and driving away Betty was finally able to talk. "Okay, sister dear, what did you put in that note?"

Nancy laughed aloud. "Oh just a little ditty I thought of at intermission. It's taken from a Selleck Osborn poem:

> "My father, sir, did never stoop so low.
> He is a gentleman, I'd have you know.
> Excuse the liberty I take,
> No longer shall my sister be wooed.
> Pray why did not your father make,
> A gentleman out of you?"

"Oh for goodness sakes! I'll never be able to go to the bank again!" Betty wiped a tear of laughter and pain from her eye. She considered the statement true. Mabel would have to take the deposits. And cash Betty's paycheck. "I should have told him I had a headache. After all this, it's almost true."

"Wait until you see who Alice hired as bookkeeper and is living down the hall from me... and her. He usually cooks breakfast on Sunday morning. You think you have a headache now..."

The girls awoke and dressed for church the next morning. Luckily, Betty could wear one of Nancy's dresses and not the outfit worn to the movie theater. Ten years older, Alice was taller than Betty and Nancy. She carried her weight with dignity. When they walked into the dining area, Alice and a middle aged man were seated at the table, drinking coffee. The Sunday morning paper lay open to a page with advertisements. The man struggled to his feet to greet the young ladies.

"Good morning! My, my, what beautiful girls we have in this room!" He grasped a cane and walked around to Nancy. "Well, introduce us, dear. I been wanting to meet *this* Nugen sister."

Betty stood uncomfortably with the man holding her hand while Nancy looked on. She couldn't bear to look into his face and instead glanced at her sisters. Both had small grins on their faces which made Betty even more distraught. Just at the moment she began pulling her hand away from the clammy grip, he released her and returned to his seat.

"This is Hubert G. Cleveland, Betty. He's the new bookkeeper for the business and brought the Buick into the fleet. Have a seat and some breakfast. He's a surprisingly good cook."

"Fleet?" Nancy asked mischievously. "The fleet of three, now with the Buick. I do enjoy driving it!"

Betty couldn't move. Some force of dread caused her to be unable to stay in the room. The smell of aftershave turned her stomach. "I...I'm not hungry. Thank you anyway. That headache from last night is returning. I'd best go lie down. Excuse me."

She hurried from the dining room and up the stairs to Nancy's bedroom. There she sat on the bedside shaking and wiping her hands on the bed cover. Betty wasn't sure what she felt, but she was sure about feeling uneasy in Hubert's presence. She tried not to think of his cold, clammy hand. Instead, she thought of his loud aftershave smell and sneezed.

"AAAHHHHCCCHHHOOOOO!"

"Bless you!" Nancy called from the kitchen.

"Goodness gracious alive, we heard that all the way down here! Sounded just like grandma!" Alice yelled.

Betty let herself fall backward onto the bed. She didn't know what to do, but had to find the strength to face the day.

Chapter Five

Betty was tired of the cold and wet winter weather of January 1940. The after Christmas sale was over at the Five & Dime and Betty was caught up with her work. One morning, a customer came in around mid-morning to purchase a sewing kit to mend his suit pants pocket. After he left, Betty noticed he left a newspaper on the counter. She saw it was from Pittsburg Pennsylvania with the front page covering the war in Eastern Europe. Not having ever seen a paper from so far away, and in an attempt to find some good news, she turned the pages to a random page.

A large advertisement caught her eye. A photo of a diesel powered railroad engine spewing smoke in a lovely valley. "Take a winter holiday to New Orleans," she read aloud. The schedule showed the train would go through Cincinnati, Ohio, Louisville, Kentucky and Nashville, Tennessee on its way south. The advertisement boasted one could travel from Ohio to New Orleans in twelve hours.

Betty sighed. The thought of travel both frightened and excited the young woman. She was still not fond of the idea of marriage. At least to anyone she had met so far. She feared her standards were too high. All her sisters had married save Nancy, who was engaged to a man named Denver she met in Oak Hill. "I wonder..." she said softly.

"Wonder what, dear?" Mabel asked. She saw the open paper. "Great day in the morning, from here to New Orleans in less than a day? Interesting they have no prices listed."

"I guess if you have to ask, you can't afford it." Betty said sadly.

"What's wrong with you today?"

"Oh, nothing. Maybe it's the after Christmas lull that's got me down. And the thought of these dresses in this other ad." Betty pointed to an image of a woman in a slimly styled outfit which was apparently high fashion. "Look how short that skirt is. Why it barely covers her knees. I could never wear anything like that. Besides, look at the price!"

"Poppycock. You have a lovely figure. And that's up there in Pittsburg, where senator and lawyer's wives shop. Though, that $19.95 price is a bit steep. In fact, I've been meaning to tell you, my daughter has, well, let's say she has outgrown some of her clothes after having that second grandchild. There will be a large box of very nice clothing here this weekend. We'll bring it out to you after church on Sunday."

"That's very nice of you. I feel so…it isn't really something I can describe," Betty said. She turned the paper to another page. "Oh, look at this story." She read. "A British warplane was pursued by two German Messerschmitt fighters over German territory. The dog fight resulted in the Brit plane falling in flames to the ground only a few miles from the German /Belgium border. It is assumed the pilot perished in the crash or was taken prisoner by the Nazis." Betty looked at Mabel. "Do you think such fighting would ever happen here in America?"

"Heavens, no. We're too far away. But all this separationist talk about not getting involved in this war is just plain stupid. Someone has to stop both Russia and Germany and it's beginning to look like we're going to have to do it." Mabel turned the page. "Oh, look at this one." The two women read silently about how two Army airmen were flying in a blizzard over Pennsylvania when something went wrong with their engine. The co-pilot bailed out, successfully parachuting to the ground. But the pilot landed the plane in what he thought was an open field of snow, his wheels dug into the ground and the

48

aircraft came to a stop upside down in a cornfield. Miraculously, the pilot survived the crash. "Now, that's USA style, there. Get the job done and walk away."

"That pilot must have been very brave, and skilled. Mabel, I wonder if maybe I should try to become a nurse's aide."

"You certainly have the stamina and heart for that kind of work. Have you thought about the hospital in Oak Hill?" Mabel put her hand over Betty's on the counter. "Isn't that nice sister-in-law of yours a nurse over there? You can't work here forever."

Betty looked up at the older woman and considered her statement. "Yes, Katherine. She is a born nurse. But, I can't leave mother. Everyone else is gone and as soon as Paul graduates, he's going in the Army. That Selective Service act is going to get him anyway. This way he can maybe get a better post like Nathan did. And Papa, well, he's not been so well lately."

"Your sense of duty to your parents is admirable, dear. But you must live your own life." The panic on Betty's face caused Mabel to pause. "Tell you what. Let's rearrange the fabric bolts and you pick out a pattern. I'll make you one of those shockingly short dresses! For the cost of that one outfit in the paper I can make a whole trousseau!"

"Oh, Mabel, you're a stitch! Ha! I made a pun! And I certainly don't need a trousseau." Betty laughed, as her long time boss rolled her eyes. "Tell you what. We made an extra-large batch of apple butter this fall. I'll trade you some for your help."

Mabel looked up in the air as if thinking. "Red. Yes, apple red colored fabric." She returned her gaze to her employee and friend.

"Red? I don't know—a *red* dress?" Betty's eyes were wide.

"Yes, red. Anything goes, these days. Come on, girl. I've got just the thing." Mabel grasped Betty's arm and pulled her away from the newspaper. "You'll look beautiful in red. I just know it."

Easter Sunday of 1940 brought the Nugen family together for church and a meal. The married daughters brought dishes to help Ethel lay out the spread. The men set up sawhorses on the back porch and placed planks of wood over them to make a long table. The "good" tablecloths were retrieved from the cedar chest and placed over the makeshift top. Children ran about, men smoked cigarettes and the women bustled about to lay out a good feed.

Betty did her part cleaning the porch Saturday evening after work. Nancy made a pass through the kitchen in preparation for the invasion of family. The two sisters walked in the grass outside the cabin toward an old, wooden shed next to an apple tree yet to come into bloom.

"Looks like that tree's about to bust out in blooms." Betty observed. "Remember when we would sit up there on the roof and eat the apples?"

"Oh, my, yes. I can still feel the belly ache after eatin' those green apples. It's truly a wonder I didn't roll right off the roof and break my neck!" Nancy answered.

"That's right! And we'd pitch the cores over in the hog pen. Say, I wonder if that little tree looking thing in the fence is an apple tree?" Betty observed.

"Well, it would certainly have had enough fertilizer! Ooh, and after we slopped those nasty old hogs we'd run down to Laurel Creek to wash and swim," Nancy mused.

"Yes, in our underwear! Couldn't do that now with those McKinney boys around," Betty laughed. "They're a mess, but awful entertaining."

"Fanny having three boys in a row has gotta be driving her crazy. It is too bad about that Les, what is it that's wrong with his eye?"

"They call it a 'lazy eye' but it doesn't slow him down any. He's sharp as a whip. With all the amazing things I see in the news, maybe the doctors can do something about it someday."

"That would be somethin', though I don't think I'd want any doctor cuttin' on my eyeball!" Nancy exclaimed with a shudder.

"It does sound…look, there's Fanny waving. The kids must be fed and now it's our turn." Betty began walking toward the house before noticing Nancy hadn't moved. "What's the matter?"

"Papa. Look how slow he's walking from the barn."

The young women watched their father for a moment. He noticed them and picked up the pace, standing a little straighter as he walked. Two of the McKinney boys ran to their grandfather and pulled him toward the house. Nancy sighed.

"He's just tired," Betty offered.

"He's tired all the time these days." She sighed again. "His legs…" She shook off the sadness and changed the subject. "Say, can I borrow that red dress of yours this weekend? It's very stylish, you know. And, I actually got some nylons. Well, actually they're rayon, but still they're stockings. Denver and I are going dancing!"

Betty looked at her sister closely. The thought of wearing stockings and going dancing had never occurred to her. "Sure, I'll get it before you leave. Stockings? That's pretty high class, sister!" Betty tried to cover her feelings of jealousy and hurried back to the cabin to join the others.

Chapter Six

Unusually cold weather in May caused Betty to worry about a frost threatening the apple crop. It also made for a cold ride into Fayetteville in D.L.'s open car. She had packed away her heavy coat. The apple blossoms, green grass and a new calf had been born safely in the barnyard. She had been sure spring had sprung, so the cold air was a surprise.

"Here, wrap up in this." Ethel threw a knitted shawl over Betty's shoulders before she left the cabin. She grasped the shawl tightly walking down the hill.

While warming her hands on a cup of hot tea in the back room of the Five and Dime, Betty heard a commotion in the front of the store. She rushed out to find Mabel and two other obviously upset women waving the arms and rattling a newspaper.

"Betty, Betty! Come here! My good Lord! Come look at this story! Two girls were murdered in Pennsylvania by a man in a tan car!" Mabel fanned her face with the paper. "Jean, here, saw a tan Chevrolet car come through town this morning. You stay inside today, girl. There's a murderer on the loose!"

Confused, Betty approached the women and accepted the newspaper thrust into her hands. The "Free Lance Star" from Fredericksburg, Virginia front page displayed a disturbing photo of several young women. The shocking headline, "Hunt Sex Maniac For Two Murders" caught her attention. The word "sex" was vulgar to her eyes, having never even heard it said aloud.

"This is disturbing, but, Mabel, there has to be hundreds of tan motor cars between here and…where does this say…" She referred back to the paper. "Bellefonte, Pennsylvania. That's a long way from here, you know."

Girl With a Star Spangled Heart

"It said a poor girl was savagely beaten two days ago! And these modern cars can travel hundreds of miles in two days!

Mabel braced herself on the counter. "He could be right here in Fayetteville!" Mabel's eyes were wide with panic. Betty patted her arm and studied the story more closely.

"It is awful. But it's very unlikely anybody like that would be around here or want any of us," Betty said.

Mabel sighed. "Goodness gracious, girl. You have no idea how pretty you are, do you? Nonetheless, we're stickin' together for the next few days, or until we hear this maniac has been captured. I'm puttin' my foot down on that!"

"Oh, Mabel...don't be so..." Betty stopped short when what appeared to be a whirlwind came in the front entrance.

"BETTY!" Nancy cried. "Oh, Betty!" She ran into her sister's arms.

"My lands, girl, whatever is the matter?" Mabel asked, hurrying to the sisters. Nancy pulled away and took a deep breath.

"Oh, it was terrible. I was at the gas station, you know the one about half way between here and Beckley?" Nancy paused to catch her breath. "The station owner's kid there was cleaning the Buick's windshield when all of a sudden a car came barreling toward us!" She swung her arms toward Mabel. "Tires were squealin' and it was goin' so fast it was out of control." Nancy took another break.

"So what happened? Why are you so upset?" Betty asked.

That car barely missed the front of the Buick and crashed into a parked truck!"

54

"Dear me! But you're not hurt are you?" Mabel queried. "Come on back here and let's sit a spell."

The women moved to the office where Betty helped the shaking Nancy into a chair. She perched on the edge of the desk.

"All right, continue the story..."

"Right. Nothing hit me or the Buick, thank goodness. Alice would flail me. But right after he smashed into that other car, here came four or five police cars with their lights and sirens blaring."

"Police!"

"Yes, and...and this guy stumbled out of his car. He had a gun in his hand! The owner's kid said, 'Git down!' and then he dove under the car! I do declare I was scared out of my mind."

"I expect so! What about the police? What happened then?" Mabel asked.

"Well, best that I could tell from my point of view, one of 'em was hunched down beside the Buick. I heard him breathing! I thought, Lord don't let him start shooting and sunk even further down in the car. I didn't see it, but, one of the police sneaked around the crashed car and tackled the guy!"

"Gracious sakes alive!" Mabel was captivated.

"The copper-policeman by the car stood up and I saw two or three uniforms on top of the guy. They were so close to the Buick I nearly fainted!"

"I thought you were hunched down," Betty said suspiciously. "Nancy, are you making all this up?"

"No! Well, I had to see what was happening, didn't I? Jeepers, that bad guy looked right at me when they walked him to the police car. And you know what? One of the police told me that guy runnin' from some crime he committed in Virginia!"

"Lordy mercy. Betty, get that paper." Betty hurried to the front and returned with the newspaper. "Nancy, was that guy in a tan car?"

"Yes, ma'am. It was kind of light brown. I guess you'd call that tan. A Chevrolet, I think. Why?"

After Mabel showed Nancy the newspaper article, the young woman truly became light headed. She turned so pale, Betty knelt before her sister to chafe her wrists. After a minute, tears fell from both sisters' eyes, releasing the tension of the previous few minutes.

Nancy looked again at the newspaper. "A murderer? Rapist? Oh, my goodness gracious. No wonder he looked so...so... scary."

"So, that means I can now safely walk the streets of Fayetteville, right Mabel?" Betty asked mischievously.

"I suppose, but let's not talk of street walking, if you don't mind."

"Oh, Mabel!"

Nancy watched the exchange between the women and added, "No one would pick her up in that old dress anyway. Betty, we've got to get you something nicer to wear."

"Not necessary. There's no reason to impress anyone. Besides, I might not need...well, never mind. Mabel, let's pump some coffee down this kid and get her back to her taxi," Betty laughed. "Working on the streets!"

Hubert G. Cleveland sat leaning back in the desk chair with one foot propped on a three legged milk stool. His right leg was stiff and without a knee joint after taking a few rounds of fire from a German machine gun in 1917 during the Great War. The field doctors in France did what they could, and by the time he arrived at a hospital in England the damaged joint couldn't be repaired. The doctors positioned the bones and allowed the tissues to fuse together. He explained it in great detail to Betty and Nancy shortly after he arrived at the taxi business.

Betty had noticed how he seemed uncomfortable unless the leg was propped up on something. She still couldn't abide his presence, but was force to when visiting Nancy and Alice. He usually sat on the edge of the chair with his leg wherever it could rest.

The milk stool had been his mothers, used on the family farm where he grew up in Virginia. He enjoyed the farm life and admired the Nugen farm. And the daughters. He and Alice had a business agreement. She wasn't interested in any other type relationship, but recognized Hubert's talent with numbers and liked his big Buick. Taking up a framed photograph, he peered at the image of Betty in the formal dress and nodded. The steer in the photo was prime, too. He heard footsteps. Alice. Placing the frame back on desk, Hubert turned back to his ledger.

Directly after graduation from high school in May of 1940, Paul Nugen announced to the family he was getting married and joining the Army Air Corps—in that order. Betty was excited for him. His long-time sweetheart fully supported the decision as most everyone in the country believed war was imminent.

All the papers carried the story of Congress passing a law entitled "Burke-Wadsworth Act" which was the first peacetime military draft conscription in the United States. Paul didn't wish to be forced into being a foot soldier when the USA entered the war, and instead aimed to learn something in the aircraft industry he could use later to support a family.

Often, Betty thought of her brothers in the Service. The boys faithfully sent money to their parents from points all around the country. She feared for their safety, especially since reports from Europe spoke of intense attacked on England and Hitler claiming to be ready to take on the USA.

Betty also indulged in more please musings of what the mountains of Oregon and Colorado looked like and how it felt to have one's toes in the salty water of the ocean. The cold, spring-fed Laurel Creek with its fresh water was exhilarating in summer, but a sandy beach with warm seawater caressing one's skin seemed quite enticing.

Yet life trudged on in Fayetteville. Franklin Delano Roosevelt was re-elected for his third term as President on November 5, 1940. The country braced for war. When Nancy stopped at the Five and Dime, she told Betty of the newsreels at the theater depicting many of the same type images of the bombing in London and German aggression they had seen in the theater the year before.

She also described a short film with a new cartoon character named Bugs Bunny and a little hunter with a big gun and a speech impediment called Elmer Fudd. Betty thought it odd to have such opposite types of films, but also recognized one could not bear to have bad news constantly.

Alice often brought Hubert to the farm where he spoke at length with Robert and spent a lot of time eating and complimenting Ethel's cooking. Betty stayed outside, as far away from him as possible. Robert's leg ulcers kept him inside much of the time, so he enjoyed Hubert's company. Ethel took a liking to the man, despite Betty's protests. She chided Betty saying her prattle unseemly and discourteous to a man afflicted with a war wound and in their older sister's employ.

Betty recognized Ethel was very proud of Alice for owning a business and providing employment for several persons, including a man. She hoped, some day, to gain that approval with her life. She knew her mother considered Hubert a good match for Alice, but Betty also knew her older sister wanted nothing to do with another marriage. Abandoned when she was pregnant with her son, Alice filed for a very quiet divorce and moved to Beckley to begin a new life. Her taxi business was going well, especially after Hubert's contribution of the 1938 Buick.

Betty waved at Alice, Nancy and Hubert drove away from the farm before turning back to the dishes. Robert walked toward the barn to check on the animals. Ethel picked up a towel to dry the plates. Neither saw Robert collapse onto the ground. An hour later, when he hadn't returned, Ethel became concerned.

"Have you seen your father?" She asked.

"No, mama. He went to the barn, didn't he? Maybe he's resting there."

"Maybe. You'd best go fetch him. He needs to get off those legs before they start bleeding."

Just a few steps away from the house Betty screamed. "Mama! Mama! Come quick!"

Ethel hurried out to where her husband lay crumpled and still. Kneeling, she pressed her fingers against his neck. "Alive. Thank God." Betty grasped Ethel's other hand, as the woman turned toward her daughter.

"Go down and get Fanny. Have D.L. bring the car. Hurry!" Ethel instructed. Betty ran the half mile distance to her sister's house as quickly as she could.

When Betty arrived breathless at Fanny's house, the entire family converged on her. As she caught her breath, all she could manage to say was, "Daddy…fell." All the McKinney's quieted. Fanny turned to D.L.

"Everybody! In the car. We're going up the hill," she said urgently. They all knew if Ethel had panicked, something bad was happening.

Chapter Seven

As 1940 drew to a close, snows fell in the mountains. Robert remained indoors after the doctor said he had suffered a heart attack and was lucky to be alive. Betty and Ethel took care of his every need. However, his life was outside, on the farm and he wilted without the touch of the animals' breath on his hand and the feel of the earth beneath his feet. Fanny's boys came up to the farm after school to do the chores Betty couldn't manage to do after she got home from work in the evening. She and the boys often had a cup of hot tea together before they went home.

A bond formed between Betty and the middle child, Les, during those evenings. His intelligence shined in the one eye which could look straight at her. He sometimes would bring his homework and stay behind to sit with his Aunt Betty. She had a good understanding of basic mathematics, but Les went far beyond what she could comprehend. Yet no one else would listen to him; no one else saw the talent and intellect within the twelve year old. Betty made herself a promise to help the boy achieve what no one in the family had done: pursue a university education.

A long and hard winter was upon West Virginia in early 1941. Snows hampered activity on the Nugen farm, yet the animals needed care and water had to be fetched from the well. Betty watched as her father's health failed to the point he could not even walk to the barn. The chores weighed upon her, though Les and his brothers helped when they could make it up the hill. Bringing in milk from the evening milking, she noticed Robert sitting on the edge of the bed. He motioned her to come nearer and patted his hand on the quilted bedspread. When she sat beside him, he took her hand in his.

61

"Betty Irene. This Hubert, you know he asked for your hand in marriage," he whispered. Betty's head dropped and she sighed. "You do not want the match." It wasn't a question.

"Oh, Papa. I haven't much hope, but, he..." She shuddered. Looking directly at her father she found the words. "I would rather stay here with you and mama. No, Papa, I do not want him as a husband. It is...well, it doesn't appeal to me in the least."

Robert chuckled. "We shall see. I suspected as much. You know your mother likes the man and wants the match. But the world is in turmoil and there may be something for you out there. Maybe somewhere besides here."

"Oh, no, Papa. I couldn't leave home," Betty cried.

"Go on, now and attend to the milk. We shall see. I have to lay down for a bit."

The next morning, February 11, dawned exceedingly cold. Ethel rose with her breath fogging in the chilled air, tending to the fires and breakfast as usual. Betty readied herself for the frigid trek down the hill to ride into Fayetteville with D.L. He was good about taking her to town on Saturday, as it was an excuse for him to have coffee at the diner with his friends. Usually, Nancy picked her up when the store closed.

"Bye, mama. I'll just step in and tell papa bye."

Ethel grasped her arm, pulling her away from the door. "He's sleeping. Leave him be." Nodding, yet confused at her mother's gruff manner, Betty left the cabin. After her daughter left, Ethel sat at the small table with her head in her hands and cried. No one ever saw the woman in tears and no one would. She shook off the emotions, stoked the fire and made a batch of biscuit dough before walking down the hill to Fanny's. Robert lay dead and she had arrangements to make.

Just after the noon hour struck on the German cuckoo clock above Mabel's desk, the front door of the dime store burst open. The bells on the handle jingled frantically, as two boys practically fell over each other struggling to get inside.

"Slow down, there, fellas! Where's the fire?" Henry Hammer joked.

Les jerked to a stop and grabbed the other. "Sorry, Mr. Hammer. Aunt Betty. We need to get Aunt Betty!" The boy's tone halted Hammer's laughter.

"What on this green earth is going on up here?" Mabel and Betty emerged from the office.

"Les? Buck? What—?" Betty stopped short. "What is it? What's wrong?" She approached her nephews. The younger, Buck, ran to throw his arms around her.

"Mama sent us to bring you. Bring you to...the funeral parlor. Oh, Aunt Betty! Grandpa's dead!" Les cried. He also too grasped hold of his Aunt. Mabel led the little group to the office where Betty fell into a chair.

"I—tried to say—say goodbye this morning. But mama stopped me. She grabbed me and pulled me away. Good Lord above, he must have—must have passed in the night." Betty turned toward Mabel. "She didn't even let me say goodbye. They came all the way in to town and didn't tell me he was gone!" She fell into tears. Mabel knelt next to the young woman and wept with her.

Suddenly, the bell on the front door rang again and was shortly followed by the sound of running across the wooden floorboards toward the office.

"Betty! Oh, Betty!" Nancy ran to her sister and the fell onto the floor sobbing. After the initial wave of emotion passed, Betty whispered in her sister's ear, "She didn't even tell me. Didn't let me say goodbye." Nancy gripped her sister's hand and looked into the blue eyes now bloodshot and puffy from crying.

"I know, sweetie. I'm not surprised. She's like that, you know." Nancy sighed and smoothed Betty's hair. "Come on, let's get over to the place. Everyone should be there soon. I came straight here after Fanny called us."

The months following Robert's death passed in a blur. Working in town and the chores at the farm exhausted Betty to the point she hadn't seen Nancy in weeks and even skipped church a few times to catch up on her sleep. Fanny sent Les and Buck up the hill almost every day to help. Both boys grew three inches that summer and developed muscles enough they handled all the heavy work.

One Saturday in September, much of the family gathered to celebrate one of the elder sister's birthday, as her husband had joined the service and was stationed somewhere in the Deep South. Throughout the summer Alice and Hubert frequently visited the farm. In fact, they became regulars at the Sunday dinner table. Betty did her best to avoid the man, but he managed to sit next to her often. It was expected for her to place a stool beneath his unbending leg. She moved around to the kitchen to clean up after the apple pie was served to get some air. Betty's ears perked up when she heard Hubert talking.

"We should sell off much of the acreage and keep only fifteen or so for the milk cow, a steer or two, and the hogs. Chickens and hogs appear to be the best investment and most efficient commodity—we do our own processing, sell chicken eggs, keep the family fed and sell the rest. After Betty and I—is that thunder? There wasn't a cloud in the sky earlier!"

"Aunt Betty! Come quick!" Les yelled from outside.

Betty hurried past Hubert and out the screen door. "What is it, Les?" She asked, wiping her hands on a dish towel.

"Planes! Hundreds of 'em!" Buck said excitedly.

"Not hundreds, goofy. But I bet there's twenty-five or thirty! "Come on!" Les grabbed his aunt's hand and pulled her out into the yard. The three stood peering into the bright blue sky with their mouths gaped open. A mass of black spots approached from the south, going north. As they got closer Les counted thirty airplanes.

"Lookie! Oh my, some of 'em have four engines! Just listen to 'em!" Buck cried.

"Those are B-17s, boys. Must be going to Washington for that Lend-Lease program with Great Britain. For the war in Europe. They have big machine guns and can drop an enormous amount of bombs." Betty spoke with confidence, until she felt a hand on her elbow. She turned sharply at the unwelcome touch and found Hubert standing much too closely. He leaned in close to her ear.

"You sure looked pretty there in the kitchen. Right at home," he whispered.

"And look at the odd tails on those three over there. They're different but have four engines, too. What are they, Aunt Betty?" Les asked.

Betty shaded her eyes to peer at the airplanes Les had pointed out, using the opportunity to step away from Hubert. "B-24's, I do believe. The 'Liberator' they're calling it. Aren't they something?"

"How does a simple, little farm girl like you know about such things? Shouldn't you be helping your mother in the kitchen?" Hubert's tone caused Betty to turn slowly toward him. She noticed Alice and her mother were standing nearby. With her right hand on Les' shoulder she steeled herself to speak.

"I can read. We get the Charleston newspaper at the store and sometimes see the Free Lance Star out of Virginia."

"Yeah, Aunt Betty knows all about airplanes and that kind of stuff!" Buck added. Hubert snorted and rolled his eyes. Les drew his shoulders up as if he were going to say something but Betty patted him lightly to signal to be still. He took up a post on her right side.

"Poppycock. Women should concentrate on women's work and not reading or war. Come on, let's go back in the house, Betty."

Standing very still, the young woman felt Buck move to stand on her left. The three faced Hubert. After breathing deeply, Betty spoke. "Aircraft will be the key to defeating Hitler whether with British or American crews. Reading about them is interesting to me. You can go in the house, if you wish. You cannot tell me what to do, sir." She looked straight at Hubert's shocked face and spoke loudly, so everyone could hear. "And don't you ever touch me again. Ever. Come, boys, let's go check on the new piglets. Race you to the barn!"

The McKinney boys took off running with Betty only slightly behind. She stopped to see what was happening after her outburst. She saw Hubert hobbling into the cabin with Alice stopping by their mother. Ethel remained still, seemingly unmoved by any of the conversation. Betty sneaked up closer to listen to what Alice had to say.

"Mother. She can't go on acting like a child, running barefoot through the grass. It isn't—"Alice stopped short as her mother raised her hand.

Ethel rocked a few times before rising to her feet. "Let me deal with it. Don't upset the apple cart."

"But it's getting' to the point there is no apple cart, mama! Maybe not any apples at all! Hubert is our only hope!"

"God will provide, child. He will show the way." Ethel turned to her most independent daughter. "Look at you, would you? Your success proves the Lord works in mysterious ways. He will show us the way. There is always hope."

Alice stared after her mother. The old woman always spouted such religious clichés when she was at a loss of what to do. Shaking her head side to side, Alice followed Ethel quietly.

Chapter Eight

A few days later, Betty considered the conversation she had with Ethel after the birthday party. It reran in her mind.

"Betty Irene, often we have to do things we don't want to do," Ethel said, as she rocked in her chair.

"But mama! This is marriage! It's my life. I simply will NOT marry that man."

"Don't sass me, girl. There just isn't much choice now, is there? What else will you do, pray tell?"

It was as if she had no say in the matter. Everyone expected her to marry Hubert. Marry him? She couldn't abide being within arm's reach of the man. All her sisters were married, or engaged, and most had children. There were no other prospects of marriage in Fayetteville, as most young men had joined the service to be able to send money home to their families.

War seemed inevitable. Every day the news was filled with stories of Germany invading countries, and, in the USA, metal, paper and rubber drives were occurring. Betty assumed the resources were for the manufacture of airplanes, tanks, trucks, and ships.

Betty saw numerous photographs in newspapers of the devastation the bombing of England and Europe. Earlier in 1941, she read an article stating Westminster Abbey had been severely damaged.

With problems like these in the world, her being twenty-three years old and unmarried seemed unimportant. She knew the love of family, but had never experienced a romantic relationship. Thinking of her brothers in the service, she wondered what she should do with her life. The farm operations had been scaled down to only what the McKinney boys could handle.

Betty wasn't really needed anymore at the family place. But answer to her mother's question was veiled by a dark curtain. Life awaited. Betty Irene Nugen did not know what it would bring. In the meantime, she had to keep working and make as much money as possible. Even her brothers in the service were consistently sending money home keeping both Ethel and Fanny stocked with flour, cornmeal and other staples. The Nugen boys serving in the armed forces seemed to be doing very well.

Betty unfolded the note to her Nathan put in his last letter. After reading it, she was thankful Ethel hadn't.

> Dear Betty,
>
> Everything is as well as can be. Nancy wrote about your situation with Hubert and mentioned mama was pressuring you for lack of other options.
>
> My suggestion is that you move in with Katherine in town. You can keep each other company and it will be easier to get to work at the Five and Dime. The house has running water and indoor plumbing—all the modern conveniences!
>
> Katherine has agreed to this and I think it would do you both good. Just contact her and let me know how it goes. I hope this helps you, little sister. Also, keep your eyes open for the news of an auxiliary in the Army. There's word they're going to let women join the armed forces.
>
> With love,
>
> Nathan

Katherine, having married Betty's favorite brother, held a special place in the Betty's heart. Gracious and gentle, her sister-in-law was like a queen. She had grace and style of the type Betty had never before seen. Moving to town sounded like a good idea. She wondered if Nathan's house had electricity. She never had what most people called "modern conveniences."

"A women's auxiliary? That could be interesting..." she said to herself.

Twenty-three years in a three room log cabin would seem like too much to some, but the farm was Betty's home. Her grandparents and father were buried on the hill. She couldn't see getting very far from home, but a winter in town with Katherine was appealing. Betty decided to tell her mother after church on Sunday she was moving out. In the meantime, she considered her small wardrobe, mostly still homemade skirts and dresses, should fit in a knapsack Paul left behind. She would wear the only pair of shoes she owned to walk away from the only home she'd ever known.

The first week of December, the Oak Hill theater was showing "They Met in Bombay" starring Clark Gable and Rosalind Russell. Nancy insisted on picking Betty up after work on Saturday and driving to Oak Hill to see the film. The newsreels before the movie started were very disturbing. A long line of strange armored vehicles appeared on the screen with the narrator stating the Japanese were pushing into Mainland China. The English could not seem to stop them. The British Empire was fighting for its very existence.

Nancy sighed when Clark Gable appeared with a top hat, white shirt and that rakish smile for which he was so famous. Gable was playing a master jewel thief out to steal the most

70

prized piece of jewelry in India. The necklace was owned and worn by a Baroness and was very tightly guarded. He was getting close to stealing the necklace until Rosalind Russell, with her alabaster skin and dark, luxurious hair appeared to do her own bit of thieving.

Nancy stuck an elbow in Betty's ribs and whispered, "We could fix your hair like that, you know." Betty nodded and continued watching the movie.

When Clark Gable put on the English captain's uniform and stood up to the invading Japanese, Betty was captivated. When he ran up the side of a hill to throw grenades on the attacking forces, she tensed in her seat and let out a slight cry when he was hit by a bullet. His eyes, the mustache, his demeanor impressed her. No one like that was around West Virginia, she was sure. Kicking herself for dreaming such nonsense, she cheered when the thief went straight and faced his punishment with his new bride by his side. The two dark haired people seemed to fit together well.

On the way back to Katherine's house, Betty wondered if there was a man to fit with herself. Not a Clark Gable, but a real person. After considering the point, she realized there was more to the world than Oak Hill and Fayetteville and wondered what was out there.

Nancy stayed with Betty and Katherine and joined the whole family at church on that cold Sunday morning. Everyone returned to Katherine's for Sunday dinner. Ethel gladly received the cash Betty continued to give her earmarked to pay for Les' eye surgery. His intelligence was undeniable, and the school principal was helping them find a doctor who could correct his vision.

After a few minutes of sitting in Katherine's living area near the fireplace, Nancy became restless. "Let's go for a drive. Whattaya say Betty? Katherine?"

"You two go on. I have to press my uniform for work tomorrow. There are some GI's coming in with injuries. I want to take good care of them."

"GI's here? Who'd a thought? Betty?"

"I declare. Don't you ever get tired of driving?" Betty asked.

"Not a bit. I love it! The power, the wind. Come on, the heater works real good in the Buick."

"You think we could go down to the river?" Betty rose to put on her coat.

"Sure, it shouldn't be too slippery yet. That windy trail is a slow go. Every time I have to go north, it takes me forty-five minutes to cross the New River."

After their exploring was done, Nancy suggested they stop at the diner in town for a cup of coffee before she had to return to Oak Hill.

The big Buick came to a stop in front of the diner and the women walked inside. A few heads turned, a few nodded in recognition, as the men gathered around the radio for the afternoon broadcast of "Sammy Kaye's Sunday Serenade." Suddenly the radio crackled and an announcer's voice spoke hurriedly.

"From the NBC newsroom in New York: President Roosevelt said in a statement today that the Japanese have attacked the Pearl Harbor Hawaii from the air. I will repeat that. President Roosevelt says the Japanese have attacked Pearl Harbor Hawaii from the air. This bulletin came to from the NBC newsroom in New York."

For a moment people in the diner remained very still, as the trepidation of what had been feared for several years became certainty. War. Everyone in the diner, including the cook, crowded around the radio.

The regularly scheduled program resumed, so one of the men turned the dial to CBS and their "The World Today" news program. They led with the story of the attack, including several reports from Washington, London, and The Philippines with analysis by a retired military man and commentary by various newsmen.

This was a new kind of war. Airplanes dropped bombs on ships with men aboard. Betty strained to hear the bulletins, but as the word was whispered and then said aloud, they backed away from the group. War. An attack from the air. The unthinkable had occurred. War had taken to the skies and America was now involved.

Chapter Nine

Steam from the train engine filled the air. Betty stopped on the steps and looked back. Nancy and Fanny waved enthusiastically while Ethel dabbed at her eyes with a handkerchief. Beyond the wooden building were the hills of West Virginia. She wondered briefly when she would see them again. The train whistle blew loudly and someone nudged her from behind. Quickly waving goodbye to her family, Betty embarked on the biggest adventure of her life.

Hurrying into the passenger car, a porter glanced at her ticket and pointed to a row of seats. Mabel advised her to request a window seat to be able to see out, and to avoid having strangers sitting on either side of her seat. Sliding in, she straightened her skirt, sat up and looked out the window. Her family had turned away and did not see her slight wave, as the train surged and jerked into motion. She watched the town of Beckley slide by, and marveled at the train rolling through the countryside. No one sat beside her, so she relaxed. Closing her eyes, she remembered when she told her mother the news.

"When are you going to accept his proposal, Betty Irene? It's likely the best offer you'll ever get," Ethel spoke rather sternly.

Betty remained silent for a few moments, gathering the nerve to speak. Several months had passed since Hubert asked Ethel permission to marry Betty. He never asked Betty, not allowing her the opportunity to say no. She couldn't stand to be in the same room with the man.

In fact she usually sneezed when she smelled his cologne. The thought of marrying him was ridiculous. After avoiding the issue for as long as possible and investigating various options, Betty came to a decision.

Having a taxi service and a contract with the Army allowed Alice's taxi service to stay in business despite the rationing of gasoline. One Saturday in June of 1942, Nancy drove to Fayetteville to get Betty for the weekend. Mabel had saved a newspaper article for Betty, and she wanted to show it to Nancy.

Reading the daily news kept the young woman apprised of events in the war both in Europe and the Pacific. She saw the photographs featuring hundreds of aircraft being produced and shipped overseas. Every able bodied man between the age of eighteen and forty in the three county area was in the service. Paper and rubber drives along with rationing of staples such as sugar, meat and textiles triggered the conflict around the world to affect even people in rural West Virginia.

In less than twelve months from the date of the bombing at Pearl Harbor, the United States was fully committed to the war effort. The article Mabel saved for Betty showed the concern the government had for the overall management of the military organizations. In May of 1942, a law was passed creating a women's auxiliary in the United States Army. A section of that auxiliary was to be assigned to the Air Corps.

Nancy was at first somewhat shocked, but afterward understood what her sister was doing. She drove Betty to the Army recruitment office in Beckley. On the wall was a large poster of a lovely woman in uniform in front of a waving American flag showing the caption, "Are you a girl with a Star-Spangled heart? Join the WAC now! Thousands of Army Jobs Need Filling!"

Nancy turned to Betty. "Are you sure? There's no telling where they'll send you."

"It doesn't really matter. I believe this is the right thing to do."

"Well, it'll get you off the mountain, and away from Hubert."

"Maybe so, Nancy. I don't know. That's not why I'm doing this. It just seems to be the thing to do for me right now. Serve the war effort. See something besides the New River Valley. This is what should happen. I'm sure I'll be back. This is home."

The swaying of the passenger coach stopped suddenly, bringing Betty back to the present. The train slowed to a stop. A porter walked through the car announcing the name of the next stop. Paintsville. Betty took a deep breath. Shyness was preventing her from leaving the seat. She would stay on this train to Chattanooga, Tennessee.

There the Army would retrieve her and any other WAC recruits and deliver them to Fort Oglethorpe, just a few miles across the state border into Georgia. The thought of what lay ahead terrified the young woman. But determined, she swallowed the fear and stayed in her seat.

A few passengers boarded at Paintsville. The porter led an older couple to the row where Betty was staring out the window. Her purse and coat were in the seat beside her. The man cleared his throat to get the young woman's attention.

"Miss, may we join you? These seem to be our seats right next to you."

Betty, startled, mumbled and gathered her things into her lap. The older woman slid into the seat with her husband groaning, as he sank into the aisle seat.

"I'm so sorry. I didn't mean to take up—" As Betty began to apologize, the older woman spoke.

"Not at all, dear. Don't worry a bit about it."

"Yes, we hope we didn't cause you any inconvenience," the man offered.

"No, no. I don't...don't have much."

"Mr. and Mrs. Reynolds here at your service," Mrs. Reynolds offered a handshake. Betty shook her hand firmly.

"Ah, a good, solid handshake, good, good. We're just going down the track a ways to see our daughter and grandchildren in Knoxville" Mrs. Reynold said pleasantly.

"Oh, that's nice," Betty replied.

"It will be. Our son-in-law has been sent to England. He's in some secret operation of some sort."

"How interesting!"

"Oh, enough about me. Where are you going, Miss Betty?"

"Fort Oglethorpe in Georgia."

"Oh, you must be a nurse? Edwin! Miss Betty is a nurse headed to the army base!"

"No, Mrs. Reynolds. I...I am going to be a WAC."

"A what? Edwin what is she talking about?" The man scooted up in the seat to look around his wife at Betty. He nodded and grinned.

"Yes, dear. Don't you remember seeing in the paper a few months ago? A women's auxiliary in the Army. I expect the Navy won't be far behind. Best idea of the war. Free up the men to fight and let the women handle the paperwork. Good for you, Miss Betty!"

"Thank you, Mr. Reynolds. I must admit to being rather frightened."

"Naturally! All this is bound to be intimidating! Will you be regular Army or..." Mr. Reynolds stopped as the train crossed over a trestle. Betty allowed Mrs. Reynolds to lean across and peer out the window at the shallow canyon beneath the bridge. The train lurched and swayed in a distressing manner as it left the trestle and returned to solid ground.

"My lands, I'm glad that was a short bridge. I don't think my nerves could stand a long one. Now what were you saying, dear?"

Betty sat up straight. "I'm going for the Air Corps, sir. Planes and such machinery have always fascinated me. I don't think I could fly, but I want to watch them soar across the sky!"

Later in the afternoon, the train pulled into Knoxville, Tennessee. The Reynolds' gathered their things, bade goodbye and good luck to Betty, leaving very empty seats behind. Butterflies again fluttered in Betty's stomach, as the nervousness of facing the unknown alone crept in. With closed eyes, she breathed deeply to regain control. Fatigue and fear was wearing her down. Her hands shook. Wondering if she could venture to the dining car, she shifted in the seat.

"Okie dokie, train! You can get going now. Ruby has found her seat! Thank you Mr. Porter!" The woman slipped the porter a nickel, tossed her bag into the seat beside Betty and sank into the aisle seat. She looked at Betty. "Hey, there! Ruby Star's the name!" She reached across and offered a handshake. Hesitant at first, Betty looked at the woman and saw a happy, friendly face crowned with blonde curls. Her features shined with little make up and she sported a bright smile. Betty shook hands with with a glad heart. This woman looked to be a fun person to be around.

"B-Betty Nugen. Pleased to meet you, Ruby." The train jerked forward and the whistle sounded.

"Whoop!" Ruby plopped into the seat as if knocked off her feet. "Away we go, Betty! Say, where are you going?"

"Chattanooga. Fort Oglethorpe in Georgia, if I-I can stay in this seat that long." Betty fidgeted and crossed her legs. Ruby noted the old shoes and worn dress. Her eyes narrowed a bit, then opened wide.

"That's where I'm going! I went and joined the Army. You?"

The women discussed their experiences up to date of the background and criminal checks, gathering employment and character references, and the Army General Classification Test. Ruby studied Betty's letter of acceptance and orders to report for basic training.

"Looks like we're in this together, toots." She noticed Betty's shaking hand. "Girl, let us remove to the dining car and get some grub! You're shakin' like a leaf!" Ruby grasped Betty's hand and directed her through the coaches to the dining car. Betty accepted the help, as she was too terrified to move from her own seat.

Over dinner, Ruby led the conversation, eventually obtaining Betty's background and a general sense of her character. She knew Betty was a good kid, naïve and shy.

"Tell you what, toots. You and me will go through this together. I'll watch your back and you watch mine. I think we're gonna be great friends."

On the other side of the small table, Betty crossed her ankles and hid her hands. Ruby's fingertips were painted a light pink and Betty's nails were short and uneven. Betty felt Ruby was a good person, and decided she could learn from the woman.

"Yes, I think that is a good idea. That's what my sister Nancy and I did. Took care of each other." Betty observed Ruby and she were about the same age and had the same goal—the WAC. Ruby reminded Betty of Nancy, in that she was a much more outspoken and brave person than Betty had ever been.

"Thanks. Yes, I think it might help me. I'll be a friend to you, also. Let me know if there's anything you need."

"Oh, I don't want anything from you! It's just I've been off the turnip truck for a few years and you just got off. We'll make a great team." Ruby shifted in her seat. "Let's stay in here for a while, or till they kick us out!" Betty appeared shocked. "I'm kidding! But let's people watch for a bit."

Betty marveled at the waiters balancing their trays filled with glasses of water and plates of food. They seemed to pivot at the waist, their legs moving with the rocking of the train while the trays remained level in steady hands. She felt the texture of the white tablecloth expecting a stiff, starched surface, but found it to be not at all like any fabric she had seen.

"This isn't just a starched tablecloth. I thought fabric like this would stain. Do you know what it is?" she asked, running her fingers over the cloth.

"Far as I can tell, they've rubbed these table linens down with lard or some kind of oil to the point I believe the boys could use them as tents and it would shed water like a duck's back." Ruby also examined the tablecloth. "It's really convenient, though, if somebody slops some gravy, it wipes right up!"

Ruby laughed so loudly a neighboring table stared. Betty, too laughed aloud, then her eyes got wide and she took in a deep breath.

"Oh, dear. Must have gotten some pepper—I need to— AAAHHHHCCCHHHOOOOO!"

"Wow, that was the most remarkable sneeze I have ever witnessed!" Ruby looked at her companion with compassion.

The two women placed their napkins on the table and rose at the same time. "Bless you, my dear!" Ruby exclaimed. "Wow, you can really rattle the windows, can't you?" She looked around at the people staring. "What are you all looking at? We've gotta laugh! We joined the Women's Army!" Ruby stated comically.

Suddenly, the dining car inhabitants burst into a round of applause. Betty blushed while Ruby grabbed her by the arm and they escaped the car.

"Sorry about that kid. Didn't mean to get that much attention. But your sneezing added to the show!" Ruby held onto the railing in the walkway between cars. Below their feet the ground flashed by so quickly the rail road ties were not visible.

"Aw, let's get back to our seats. All this excitement is making my stomach turn flip flops," Betty confessed. "But I must confess that laughing sure did feel good!"

The women returned to their seats, they sat next to each other, leaving their purses and packages in the aisle seat.

"To discourage unwanted visitors," Ruby advised.

Over the next few hours, the women exchanged information about their backgrounds. Ruby understood why Betty seemed withdrawn and was shocked when she heard about the pressure she received to marry a man she couldn't tolerate.

"I do believe you made the right decision, honey. That man sounds downright awful!" Ruby reached over and squeezed Betty's forearm. The women's eyes met and each felt an understanding of the other. A bond was formed at that moment which would endure for a lifetime.

Ruby could type fifty-five words per minute on the Underwood in the office where she had served as secretary to bank president in her home town of Columbus, Ohio. Describing the city where she lived made Betty somewhat uncomfortable to describe her own home which had no running water or electricity. But Ruby seemed genuinely interested.

"Well, I've been living with my sister in Fayetteville for a while, but home is really out there at Laurel Creek on top of that hill. It's hard to describe, it's like the land itself is part of me. The trees are my great, great, great uncles. The grass is the same grass my sisters and brothers played in many years before I was born. The hill was there long before Columbus discovered America. It isn't much when you compare to fancy places in town, but it is my home."

Ruby looked at her companion. "Sounds divine! I don't quite get all that connection to the land and such, but it must have taken a boatload of courage for you to up and leave it."

"I don't know about that. Like I said, it was the right thing to do," Betty replied.

"Right. Maybe we ought to rest up a bit. After we stop at Chattanooga, who knows when we'll get to rest again?" Grinning, she squeezed Betty's arm again. The train rolled on, the swaying serving as a cradle which rocked the young women to sleep.

"Chattanooga – Last stop in Tennesee!" The porter called, as he walked up the aisle. Leaning toward the sleeping women he spoke loudly. "Chattanooga! This is the Fort Oglethorpe stop, ladies!"

Betty started awake and Ruby flashed the porter a smile. "Thank you, sir. The Women's Army might not appreciate having to pick us up in Birmingham! Come on Betty, let's get ready. You have your luggage ticket?"

Betty stared. "Luggage? Oh, all I have is this one little case and my pocketbook."

"That's all? My lands, girl. We're going to have to go shopping after basic training, if we ever get to wear street clothes again!"

"Well, I didn't have a lot, and I figured with the uniforms, wouldn't need much," Betty admitted.

The train rumbled to a stop and the women exited onto the wooden landing at the train station. Smoke from the train and steam from the brakes filled the air. Ruby retrieved her suitcase while Betty stood and stared at the scene.

Men and boys in uniform hurried from one place to another. Young women sniffed into their handkerchiefs while watching their boyfriends and husbands walk away. Several men in suits smoked cigars, women in high heels clicked past. Betty had never seen so many people in one place, and everyone seemed to be on their own personal mission. She sighed. Just as she was on a mission, she realized. To do what, she didn't know.

Ruby grabbed Betty's elbow and pointed toward a stern looking women in a uniform and Hobby cap just like the one on the poster Betty saw in the recruiter's office. Ovetta Culp Hobby had championed the Woman's Army Corps and was the top ranking officer. Betty knew the hat had been named for the famous woman.

She picked up her small case and walked toward the uniformed woman. Not knowing anything about rank or how to address someone in the military, she simply held out her hand in an offer of a handshake. Her hand was shaking as the woman grasped it firmly. Ruby stood by, watching.

"Hello. You would be...?" The officer asked.

"Betty I. Nugen, ma'am. I—we're going to Fort Oglesby, ma'am," Betty stuttered.

"That's right. We're gonna be WAC's!" Ruby interjected. The officer raised one eyebrow at the boisterous intrusion, glancing in the flamboyant woman's direction without releasing Betty's hand.

"Indeed. We shall see about that. Ladies, there is a small bus waiting in front of the depot. We expect several more recruits on the next train from St. Louis and then we'll be on our way to the base." She released Betty's hand. "It will be an hour or so. Go get yourself a soda or cup of coffee in the café and I'll round you up when it's time to go. It's just past the big area with the domed ceiling. I am Major Nettles. Your name?" The officer turned to Ruby.

"Ruby Star, at your service, ma'am," Ruby replied with a touch of sarcasm.

"Star?" The major consulted her clipboard. "There's no Star on this list. There is a—"

"Okay, okay, you got me. Starnowski is my real name."

"Yes, as I was saying, though I am glad you pronounced it for me. You girls go on to the coffee shop. I have to move over to the other track to meet your fellow recruits."

The two women watched as the major walked confidently in her sturdy shoes across the boards of the landing. Betty looked about with a hint of panic.

"It's okay, kiddo. Let's go see that famous dome. I read the guy who designed it won a prize for the architecture back in nineteen oh something or another," Ruby said. Betty nodded, calmed her nervousness and smiled.

"Yes, let's go see it! I think a cup of coffee sounds pretty good."

Chapter Ten

All along the road to the fort, Betty felt as though they were riding through a dense forest. The forests she knew were on hills and this part of the country was nearly flat. One couldn't see through, or above the trees. When the bus pulled through the gates, Betty's heart fluttered and she felt quite anxious. Something in her face caught Ruby's attention.

"Honey, you look as nervous as a long tailed cat in a room full of rocking chairs!"

"Shhh!" Betty didn't want any more attention.

The car stopped and the woman officer who had met them at the train station stood with a rigid back at the door of the bus.

"Ladies, you will exit and form a straight line along the painted stripe on the blacktop. You will remain there in that line until the commanding officer and myself deliver the welcome and instructional speeches." She paused for effect and to be sure everyone was listening. "When dismissed, you will walk in single file through the door labeled 'New Recruits.' Now, get moving!"

"There's no need to get your tail up and your stinger out!" a voice said softly.

Betty glanced about and saw the officer staring at one of the women as if memorizing her features for future reference. The women ducked her head and attempted to appear innocent.

"Remind me to keep my big mouth shut!" Ruby whispered.

"Oh, no. The dust…Ahhhhh Chhoooooo!" Betty let go with one of her bigger sneezes. "Oh, dear. Excuse me, please," she said to the faces looking in her direction. No one dared offer a

"Bless you." When everyone was getting their bags, Ruby again whispered to Betty.

"You might be shy, honey, but your sneezes sure aren't!"

"Oh, hush. Let's go."

After the camp uniforms had been issued, the women were led to a quonset hut. This type of building had been nicknamed "The Can" due to its appearance of being a tin can cut in half lengthwise. Betty listened closely to the instructions to claim a bunk and stow their personal and military gear in the footlocker. Some of the girls looked overwhelmed. Others were bright eyed and taking everything in. Betty considered though she would be in a room full of girls, she had her own bed and that was an improvement over sharing one bed with three sisters.

Later, the women were shown to the latrine and again Betty was glad for her experience with outhouse type restroom facilities. Some of the women were shocked at the primitive plumbing. However, the officer informed them of a newly installed gas water heater which would deliver hot water to the shower units in the bathing hut. Betty had never taken a hot shower. Only while living with Katherine was she able to take a bath in water specifically drawn for her to use.

The women settled into a routine of early rising to Reveille, marching, singing marching songs, and more marching. They took classes on bookkeeping and Army office procedures. The training they received would serve them well in the posts to which they would be assigned.

The chow hall was a new adventure for Betty. Standing in line to get a tray of food seemed extremely odd to her. The haphazard way the trays were prepared seemed sloppy and not at all a good system. She and Ruby compared notes on their experience with food service. Where Betty had only eaten at a diner or restaurant a few times, and she took a small lunch to school each day, Ruby went out to eat more times than not. Betty promised to teach Ruby some cooking and canning tricks and Ruby promised to take Betty out to eat at a fancy restaurant.

The two women found a friendship which seemed improbable. But each had experiences the other had not had, so together they could expand each other's knowledge. Life as a WAC suited them—a place to sleep, three square meals per day, and a united purpose to serve their country the best they could.

Late one Saturday evening, Betty and two other uniformed WAC trainees walked through the base after an evening of dancing in Chattanooga. Under one of the few lights they noticed a junior officer leaning on his jeep. The ladies remained in the shadows and stopped to whisper.

"Isn't that the Lieutenant who attacked one of the girls in Company C?" Betty asked.

"Yep, that's him. He's hit on me a couple of times. Bad seed type. Must have known somebody to get that rank. Or a college boy. Girls, you follow, but keep back in the darkness. Let's see what happens with Lieutenant Thinks He's Hot Stuff." Ruby sauntered away and into the light. Betty and Kate quietly walked through the gravel to a closer position. Not knowing what Ruby was up to, they stood at the ready.

"Well, well, what have we here?" the Lieutenant slurred. The man obviously had also been to town and visited a few bars. He took an unsteady step toward Ruby. "Come here, darlin'. I been waitin' for you." Tripping over his own feet, he fell into Ruby, rotating their positions, and pressed her again the jeep.

Remaining calm, Ruby spoke softly. "Now, Lieutenant, is that any way to treat a lady? Where have you been? A brewery?"

The man pressed his face into her neck, "Doesn't matter. Where I'm going is more important." He reached toward her blouse and pulled down. Bracing herself, Ruby threw a knee into his groin. As he doubled over, she raised the other into his forehead.

"Just like marching. Now!"

At the signal, Betty and Kate hurried from the darkness. Kate kicked the back of one of the Lieutenant's knees, causing it to bend forward and throw him off balance toward Ruby. He doubled over again with pain. Betty folded her hands together and brought down a forceful blow to the back of his neck that sent him to the ground.

"Wow! That was great! Where'd you learn that punch?" Ruby kicked the Lieutenant to get his attention.

Betty shook out her hands. "I grew up with lots of brothers, remember? Oh, dear, we've beat up a man." She couldn't help but giggle. "Now what?"

"Well, I believe the Lieutenant, here, well he got into a little skirmish in town over a girl and the boyfriend tossed him around a bit." She put the toe of her standard issue shoe onto the Lieutenant's cheek. "Right, sir? You certainly didn't get beat up by three WAC's, did you?" The man nodded agreement.

"Girls, it's almost curfew," Kate offered. A vehicle approached. Ruby straightened her uniform and hailed the jeep to stop.

"Hey, we were just walking by and the Lieutenant here fell right out of his jeep! Looks like someone in town might have gotten a punch or two in on him. Will you take care of him? We've got to get back to the barracks before curfew."

"Sure, honey. Say, you didn't mess him up did you?" the driver grinned.

"Us? We are US Army trained, but we'd never beat up an officer!" Ruby replied. The women linked arms and walked away. "Well, unless he deserved it," Betty said softly. Bursting into laughter, the WAC's ran to their barracks.

Graduation from basic training was anticlimactic to the women who endured boot camp. But they did get their official green wool uniforms and rank designations. When the post assignments were announce, Ruby and Betty were relieved they would be going to the same place. Many of the other women were sent to California to prepare to go overseas. Betty was secretly glad she would be stationed at Carlsbad, New Mexico, only 1500 miles from her home and not halfway around the world in New Zealand or on a Pacific Island. She certainly did not want to go to Europe after reading for years about the devastation the war had caused.

She and Ruby bade goodbye to each other as they boarded different trains for their short leave before reporting to Carlsbad. Outfitted in their full dress uniforms with Pallas Athena and US insignia, they looked sharp and felt even sharper. From then on, they were required to wear the uniform when in a public place.

Betty settled in the seat of the train which would take her home. She was now a member of the US Army complete with a set of dog tags. The thought of being a part of something so large and powerful, along with the training she received at Ft. Oglethorpe, combined to give her a confidence she had never before experienced. Betty Irene Nugen was a private in the Women's Army Air Corps.

Betty sat alone. She recognized several women from the base, but none sat with her. Each seemed to be absorbed in her own thoughts. A sea of Army green or khaki was all Betty had seen for weeks, so a navy blue with white trim uniform stood out. The woman wearing Navy insignia on her collar looked down at the seat numbers. This revealed a hat with blue rim and white crown. As her face rose, a friendly smile greeted Betty's gaze.

"Looks like this is my seat right next to you, sweetie. I've got to get off my feet, these shoes are killing me!" the woman declared as she sank into the padded seat. She turned toward Betty and stuck out a white gloved hand. "Delores is the name, promoting the WAVES is my game!"

Betty grasped the woman's hand in a friendly shake. "WAVES? That's Navy, right? I'm Betty Nugen, fresh out of Ft. Oglethorpe to be a WAC."

"Well we're in the same boat, or train as the case may be. Let me get these shoes off and we'll get acquainted."

Betty smoothed her wool skirt and considered her own shoes. Brown leather, they were the first pair of new shoes she had ever owned. Sometimes WAC graduates didn't receive their dress greens or shoes right away, but a new shipment had come in just before graduation and the ladies of Betty's group were properly outfitted.

She was glad of that, looking at the sharp Navy uniform Delores wore. Braid adorned the sleeves of the jacket and her shirt was crisp white. She peeled off the gloves, folded them carefully, and placed them in the brown leather pocketbook sitting next to the discarded navy blue pumps.

"I wonder why the military powers suit us up with all this stuff, but don't give us a proper purse to match our shoes?" Delores asked.

"I'm just glad to have the shoes…" Betty said softly.

Delores appeared compassionate and avoided responding to the comment. "Where are you headed?"

"West Virginia. Fayetteville specifically. I'm going home to see my family before being sent to Carlsbad, New Mexico," Betty answered.

"Hmm, never heard of that town. Up in the mountains?"

"Yes, ma'am. But this train goes through Charleston. My sister's meetin' me there.

"Good, good. Then we'll be together for a while. I'm headed to Washington. I have to assist a couple of the admirals with an event."

"You travel a lot?"

"Oh, yes, indeed. I've been all over this country two or three times in the past year. They need me in San Francisco. Then they need me in Washington. I'll be glad when airplanes can take us across the continent. It will be so much faster than trains." Delores shifted in her seat to face Betty.

"How interesting!" Betty exclaimed. "The trip from Beckley to Chattanooga to get to the base was the only travelling I've ever done. Have you been through Carlsbad? Do you know what it's like?"

"I think so, one time when I caught the train in San Diego we went through there. All I remember is lots of brown hills. Of course it was in late fall at the time. Much of that state is desert-like, though one can see tall mountains from time to time."

"It will be very different from home. Everything is green there, except when the snows come."

"Sure will, sweetie. In more ways than one. You're in the Army now!"

The women relaxed as the train began moving. Heads snapped backward as the train surged forward in a jerking motion. Items moved about, Delores' shoes jumped into the walkway. When she bent over to pick them up, another surge caused her head to hit the back of the next seat. Her hat, secured with pins, only shifted a little to one side. Straightening it, her calm demeanor faded.

"What's going on? Are the wheels square? The tracks have gaps in them? For goodness sake, let's get going, maybe this misery will end!"

Betty stifled a laugh, seeing the woman flustered with the situation. "You'd never make it riding in a wagon pulled by a mule, I'd say!"

Delores glanced at Betty. "Oh, I'm not that soft. Grew up on a farm in Kansas. But you'd think in time of war they could make a train behave correctly! Why did you join up and leave West Virginia?"

"It just seemed to be the thing to do. All the men were gone, I wasn't married yet, so... You?"

Delores sat back in her seat. "Married or joined up? Actually it runs together. See, I had a few dates with this handsome young man, one of two brothers who were about to ship out to England. He asked me to marry him, and I thought then, he might not come back and I can give him this to take with him. So we eloped. He shipped out, and it wasn't six months before we got the telegram he'd been killed."

"Oh, my, how horrible! Three of my brothers have gone to Europe, we pray for them every day."

"As we all do, sweetie. But I moved into Kansas City and got a job at one of the aircraft manufacturing plants. It was good money and life was going pretty well. One day, a friend asked me to stop at the WAVES recruiter to get some information for her. I agreed, and when the ensign gave me the pitch, I joined up right then and never looked back. It was a chance to get out and see things, and I wouldn't have had that opportunity working a factory job."

"So did the both of you join? You and your friend?"

"That's the funny part of the story. I took her the information and she decided not to join. Maybe it was a spur of the moment decision, but it was the best decision I could have made."

"Because of the travel?"

"That, and to help serve the war effort. Those admirals need to be planning battles, not planning parties."

Betty nodded agreement and fell silent. She still wasn't exactly sure why she had joined the Army. As if reading her mind, Delores spoke again.

"Are you in regular Army, or the Air Corps?"

"Air Corps. I have always been interested in airplanes and my friend, Ruby, can fly one. But I just wanted to serve so where I am doesn't matter much."

"Oh it will matter! Getting to see all the handsome airmen, and hear the planes fly over, I bet it will be great!"

"I do love the sound of the airplane engines. If they'd let me learn mechanicing, I'd give it a try."

Delores assessed her companion and grinned. A farm girl from the Appalachians wanted to be a mechanic! She squeezed her feet into the hated shoes. "I really must requisition a size bigger shoe this next time. Well, I'm off to the head." Betty's face appeared confused. "The head. The latrine. The water closet."

"Yes, okay. But why is it called the head?"

"I'm not rightly sure, honey, it's just Naval terminology. I'll be back in a minute. Watch my things, please?" She rose and took off without waiting for an answer. Betty smiled, seeing passenger faces watch as Delores walked down the aisle. She wondered if the heads would turn when she had to walk to the latrine.

When Delores returned, Betty made a move to rise. She smoothed her skirt and tucked in her blouse. Delores studied the young woman's profile for a bit, then rose to her feet.

"Hang on a second there, dearie. Let's fix you up a little bit."

"Why? I'm just going to the powder room."

"Maybe so…but one never knows who one might meet between here and there. Turn around, let me fix your hair." Delores took pins from Betty's curls and let them bounce free. Next, she took the garrison cap in Betty's hand, popped it open and checked the shape, then pinned it into her hair at what would be considered a slightly rakish angle. She took a can of hairspray out of her purse and pushed down a stray curl.

Betty sat up straight and drew in a breath. "Oh, oh, hold on, I'm going to... AAAHHHHCCCHHHOOOOO!"

"My goodness. Bless you dear. You have lipstick? I expect you sneezed yours off." Betty shook her head in the negative. "Okay, use this." Delores placed a compact and lipstick case into Betty's hand. Sitting back down, applied the lipstick as Nancy had taught her to do. When she looked over at the WAVE, a shocked smile appeared on Delores' face. Betty held the compact mirror out to take in her entire visage and was also surprised.

"Whooeee, that color suits you fine, Betty! Look out world, here comes Private Betty Nugen, you'd best get out of her way!"

"Oh Delores, please! You'd think Clark Gable was waiting for me to walk by."

"You think I would have come back so quickly if he'd been up there? You get out there, walk like you own the place. Keep your head up and don't worry about anything. Just notice what reaction you get. Trust me, sweetie, it feels real good."

Betty hesitantly entered the aisle, composed herself and walked away. Delores grinned as both men and women watch her pass by with nods of appreciation. She held her head high all the way to the powder room and collapsed against the door, closing it with a thud. Betty looked into the mirror over the tiny sink and saw something she hadn't seen in her reflection before. A woman looked back at her with bright blue eyes contrasting with the green of her blouse. She stood upright, saluted herself in the mirror and grinned with satisfaction.

As she exited the powder room, she came face-to-face with a woman in an officer's WAC dress uniform. The woman held up a hand as if to stop Betty from advancing or retreating. Suddenly, Betty realized whom she had encountered. Colonel

Oveta Culp Hobby, the commander of the WAC had toured the base a few weeks after Betty arrived at Fort Oglethorpe. Widening her eyes with panic, the younger woman took a step backward and saluted the superior officer.

"Relax, ma'am," Colonel Hobby said. "I still haven't gotten used to all this saluting." The woman had a strong Texas drawl which made her seem much less intimidating. "When you walked by, I thought perhaps you were an officer I hadn't met. You have a strong presence, Private—"

"Nugen, ma'am. Betty Nugen. Thank you ma'am. It is an honor to meet you," Betty's hand shook with nervousness.

"Rubbish. It is you on whom the WAC depends. The young, sharp and proud women. I am glad to have met you today." Colonel Hobby stepped aside to clear the path for Betty to return to her seat. "Where are you headed?"

"Ma'am, home to West Virginia for a week, then I'm to report to Carlsbad, New Mexico."

"Good, good. Wave at Texas for me when you pass through there. Good luck Private Nugen."

"Thank you, ma'am. Thank you." Betty nodded her head once and began walking down the aisle. After several steps she let out the breath she had held. When she reached her seat, Delores caught her as she fell forward.

"What on earth? Did you see Clark Gable after all?"

"No. Someone even more important. And more real." Betty took a deep breath and looked at her companion. "That's why you fixed me up, isn't it? You saw Colonel Hobby and thought you'd give her a show!"

"Now, don't get huffy. Sure, I saw her. Just wanted to see what a great gal she had in her ranks, that's all."

Betty reached out to touch her new friend's hand. "I'm sorry. It was frightening standing there in front of the highest ranking woman in the Army! But, thanks to you I did it. Isn't that something? You act confident and then you're confident."

"Yes, it is strange. But it works! Say, let's go to the dining car, maybe we can talk a cookie or something out of one of the stewards! But first let me squeeze my feet into these tinkerbell shoes."

Betty laughed, the sound ringing throughout the train car. Delores broke down also and the women laughed until tears streamed down their faces. Emotions, fears, trepidation, and relief found release through the joyous laughter.

Chapter Eleven

Betty and Ruby stood before a bulletin board outside the mess hall. They wore the dress greens, as Ruby had seen a notice where a photographer was offering free photo sessions to any WAC in uniform.

"Come on, I already checked with that guy in the mail room, he's going to town and will take us!"

Betty seemed hesitant. "I-I don't know, a real photographer studio?"

"Goodness gracious, how fancy can it be? It's in the metropolis of Carlsbad New Mexico right smack out here in the desert." She took Betty by the elbow. "Besides, don't you want a nice photo in your uniform to send back home?"

"Yes, it would be nice to have one. I hope they can touch up the negatives to make me look better."

"Baloney, you look beautiful. Let's go, I told him 3:00 and it's five of..."

The women hurried to another building on the compound in time to climb into the back of a mail truck driven by Ruby's friend.

"Ok, so it's not a limousine, but it's free and going where we wanna go," Ruby said when she saw Betty's amused and slightly disgusted look. The women sat on bags of mail and fought to keep their balance. Luckily, the trip only took about ten minutes, and Betty only sneezed twice. When they arrived in town, the driver pulled out a step to help the ladies to the ground.

As he left, Betty touched her friend's elbow. "How long do we have? When's he coming back?"

"Uh, well, it was a one way trip this time. He's going on to El Paso or somewhere. We'll catch ride back, don't worry."

"Famous last words. You know it's against the rules to hitchhike, and I sure don't want to walk all the way back in these shoes!" Betty declared.

"Don't worry, the Lord will provide. Isn't that what you always say?"

Betty nodded. "That's true. It's what my mama always said. Oh, let's go find that fancified studio."

After asking directions once, the women found the small photography studio facing the main street through town. A large window allowed a view into the building, and they saw a fellow WAC posing quite dramatically.

"I am not going to do that." Betty declared.

"Of course not. Just be you. I'll make some faces so you'll smile. Tell you what, I'll go first, just watch what I do."

A bell on the door announced the entry of the two women. The photographer wheeled around and stepped toward them.

"Ah, you are come to have picture taken? Good, good, just wait a moment while I take a few more of your beautiful colleague. What a beautiful day it is! The sun, the beautiful women-blonde, brunette, and the jet black, the camera. Ah, I love America!"

"He's a foreigner?" Betty whispered. Ruby pointed to the sign hanging above the small counter in the foyer. "Angelo Capillata Photographer and Pasta (After 6 pm) An Italian? Aren't we fighting against Italy?"

100

Before Ruby could speak, Angelo turned from the camera. "Bellissima, not to worry, I was born in New York City after my parents immigrated to America. They only spoke Italian so my English, it isn't so good."

"How'd you end up in New Mexico?" Ruby asked, as he helped the blonde WAC down from the platform and spoke to her.

"You come back here next Saturday? I will have the photographs for you." She agreed, nodded to the other women and left the studio. Angelo turned his full attention to Ruby.

"It's is a long and sad story. The short version is my brother convinced me we could make a fortune in mining silver. He was mistaken. But the beauty of the land captured my heart, so when he returned to New York, I stayed. I want to take beautiful photographs of nature and women, not depressing images from the city." He glanced at Betty. Who is first? You?" Angelo held his hand out.

"Oh no, take Ruby first. I'll just stand over here and watch." Betty withdrew, folding her arms over her chest.

"Ah, a shy one. Yes, Miss Ruby, let us begin."

Betty leaned against a doorway, watching Angelo pose Ruby in to different positions. A flash outside the window caught her eye. Her breath caught for a moment, seeing a tall, dark and genuinely handsome man who closely resembled the movie star Clark Gable. Quickly recovering, she noticed the man paused, as he walked past the large window. She quickly looked away.

"All right, Miss Betty. Let's have you step this a-way. Oh, my, such a blush on your cheeks! Hurry, we must get the shot and I can match the color later!"

Seating her on the stool, Angelo framed the shot and Ruby caught Betty's attention by making a funny face. The amused smile which took over her face was captured by the shutter with Angelo fluttering about stating how beautiful she looked. He took another photograph and stood back.

"Ah, the face, the skin, that dark brown hair. We need something…Take off—"

"Watch it there, mister," Ruby warned.

"Oh, no, no, just the outer jacket. The green, it not so good in the artist's eye. I need…" Angelo looked out the window and gasped. "That!" He hurried from the studio into the street. Ruby ran to the window to see what was happening.

On the sidewalk, Angelo faced an Air Corps airman and his companion. Ruby gasped.

"Oh my, is that…?"

Betty joined her at the window. "I thought so too, for a moment. He really looks like Clark Gable, doesn't he?" Just then the man in question looked up at the ladies in the window. He grinned and nodded once. Then his friend elbowed him. A short exchange occurred, resulting in the airman taking off his dark brown leather bomber jacket. Angelo ran inside with the prize in hand.

"You'd better not get perfume on it! My girl would skin me alive!" The airman cried.

"Numbskull. WAC's don't wear perfume. Look at that girl!"

Inside, Angelo was excited. He struggled with the large, heavy jacket. The two women looked at him as if he'd gone insane. But he was so intense, they both giggled a bit.

"This! This is what we need. Miss Betty! Let me slip this around your shoulders. Yes, take off the uniform jacket. Just pull this monstrosity together in the front, like this. Yes, yes, the sheepskin is perfect against your skin!" He gripped the front of the jacket and had Betty hold it in place. Running back to the camera, he looked through the lens. "Oh, dear, the hat and the tie, they must go!"

Ruby stepped up to where Betty sat and unpinned her hat, fluffed her curls, loosened the tie and unbuttoned the top two buttons of her blouse. Tucking it all within the folds of the bomber jacket, she looked at her friend. "Holy Toledo! This one is going to be great! Take the picture, Angelo!"

"Look away, out the window—at the young men. Relax your face, Miss Betty. Yes, that's better. See the airmen out there? Smile at them!"

Just then Betty's eyes met the intense blue eyes of the Clark Gable look alike. Ruby watched her friend's face soften and her lips part in a delightful smile. Following Betty's gaze, she looked out the window and saw the mystery man's face melt into a gentle grin.

At that moment, Angelo took the photograph, knowing it was a magical shot. Another pair of WAC's came in, and he motioned to Ruby, who understood she was to repair Betty to her uniform and make room for the next customers. He gently removed the jacket.

"Oh yes, this was the thing. Just what we needed. I was so tired of green!" He started to the door.

"Oh, no you don't. That coat might be our ticket back to the base. Give it to me, Angelo."

"Yes, yes, that is fine. Here, take it. Both of you fine women come back next Saturday for your photographs. But I must say, one or two of those might end up on the nose of some airplane!"

"Right. We'll see about that. I gotta hook up with a pilot first. Hey, this might be my chance. Ready, Betty? Let's go outside and meet these fellas!"

Betty followed her friend out onto the sidewalk. The two men walked up to them, the airman holding out his hands. He accepted the jacket from Ruby with a shocked look on his face. She grinned and stepped backward to stand beside Betty.

"Thank you for the use of the jacket, sir." Betty offered. "The photographer seemed to think it was just the thing. I'm sorry he confronted you like that."

"No problem, ma' am. Hey, I'm Clark Featherstone and this here is Glenn Fields." The tall man held out a hand to Betty.

"Pleased to meet you," he said softly. "This numbskull goes by the name of Tex." Betty's knees grew weak at the sound of his voice. The deep baritone seemed to wrap around her like a warm blanket. Realizing she was blushing, she looked down at her shoes. Ruby broke the momentary silence.

"Thanks! Clark, eh?" She glanced at Betty. "Clark...I wouldn't have guessed that. I think I like Tex better. I'm Ruby Star and this is Betty Nugen. Say, do you fellas have a car or jeep? We could use a ride back to the base."

"Yeah, sure, but you have to ride in back of the jeep. Can't let my girl see you with me," Tex stated.

"Again I must call you a numbskull. You can't ask these ladies to crawl in the back of a jeep in those skirts!" Glenn teased. Betty looked up and saw the humor in his face. Ruby took the challenge.

"Very true. Then, I get to drive and Betty takes shotgun. You two can crawl in the back!"

"You can drive?" Tex was skeptical.

"Of course. Heck, I can fly a plane. Did it a lot up in Saint Louie with my boss. He is a fanatic. Does all the air shows. I thought about joining the WASPS, but the WAC looked more promising...and safer."

"It's all true." Betty offered. "Ruby is an amazing woman. Where is the jeep?"

"Ma'am, allow me to escort you to our mode of transportation. I must advise you to pin on your hat. It can get a bit windy in the jeep." Glenn took Betty's elbow in his hand and guided her along the sidewalk.

With her eyes firmly on the concrete in front of her, Betty fought the fluttering she felt in her chest. Breathing softly, she calmed her heartbeat and wondered about the man attempting to match his steps with hers. She listened to him talk, sounding so sophisticated, yet down to earth. The soothing voice sank into her. Continuing to stare at the sidewalk, she almost missed his question.

"Where are you from?"

Betty looked upward and glanced at the tall man walking beside her. "West Virginia. Fayetteville."

"That's one place I haven't been. Started in Missouri and travelled to Washington state, down to California and back over to Texas, but I don't believe I've ever been east of the

Mississippi." Betty raised her eyebrows. "Oh, don't be impressed. My brothers and I were searching for work during the Depression. We picked crops all over the northwest. Then I learned masonry work with the CCC."

"Civil Conservation Corps? Wasn't that a New Deal program of Roosevelt's? You can build things?"

"Correct. Might even take that as my trade after the war. In the meantime, I type reports and letters. Here's the jeep! I believe you have shotgun, Miss Nugen." He helped her into the passenger seat. Ruby hopped in behind the steering wheel and adjusted the seat where she could reach the pedals. The men climbed over the back bumper and sank into the minimal back seat. Tex reluctantly handed Ruby the keys. She accepted them with aplomb.

"Hang on, boys, this might be bumpy ride! Betty you hold on, I don't want you falling out of this rattletrap! And away we go..." She started the engine, put the vehicle in gear, and continued to shift the gears perfectly as they gained speed. "Wheeee! This is great fun!" She yelled over the wind noise.

Behind Betty, Glenn watched her coffee brown colored curls fly in the wind. Suddenly, her garrison cap came loose and he caught it in midair. Leaning forward, he placed his arm on her shoulder. Startled, she turned to see her crumpled cap in the large, tanned hand.

"I guess it wasn't pinned on well enough for this wind...Ruby, how fast are you going?" Betty asked.

"As fast as it will go!" Ruby replied happily, but let up on the accelerator pedal a bit.

"Thank you." Betty said to Glenn, as she took the cap from his hand. He immediately withdrew his arm. She tucked the cap in the waistband of her skirt and folded her hands in her lap. Markedly aware of the presence of the man behind her in the vehicle, she sat very still. Before long they approached the base. Ruby motioned Betty to lean across the open area between the seats and listen.

"See that truck up there?" she asked into Betty's ear so the men could not hear. "I'm gonna pull over behind it and we can walk on in, okay?" At the nod of agreement, Ruby eased the jeep over to the side of the road and brought it to a stop behind a parked truck.

"What are you doing?" Tex asked.

"We'll get out here, fellas. That way your girlfriends won't give you any trouble about riding around with a couple of WAC's," Ruby offered, as she adjusted her uniform after stepping out of the jeep. Betty took out her garrison cap and pinned it in her hair. Before the men could move, the women were walking around the side of the truck.

"Let's duck behind here and listen in. That'll let 'em go on in and wonder where we went," Ruby whispered.

"You are downright devious! Okay, it would be..." The women fell silent when they heard voices.

"Girlfriends?" Glenn said. Then he stood up in the jeep, cupped his hands around his mouth and shouted, "I don't have a girlfriend!" He crawled into the passenger seat and breathed one more word. "Yet."

"How do you like that?" said Tex. "That Ruby is something else! I might just have to look her up…" He plopped into the driver's seat.

"What about this girlfriend you keep talking about?" Glenn asked with a knowing grin.

"Eh, she's pressuring me to get hitched before I go to England. I'm not so sure I want that responsibility hanging over me."

Nodding understanding, Glenn gripped the seat of the jeep as Tex pulled out into the road. They stopped at the gate to check in and to try to catch up with the women before they disappeared into WAC quarters.

"Did you see two girls walking this way just a bit ago?" Glenn asked of the MP. The guard simply shrugged with indifference. "Aw, come on, Tex, let's get back to the barracks," he said with irritation.

Tex looked closely at his friend before widening his eyes. "Don't worry, Sarge. This base ain't that big. We'll find 'em." He pressed the gas pedal and left a small cloud of dirt on the MP at the gate.

After the dust cleared, Betty and Ruby walked through the gate as nonchalantly as possible. The MP took notice, then shrugged again. The girls held in the laughter as long as they could.

Chapter Twelve

On Tuesday morning, Betty arrived at her desk for her normal day's work. A stack of postcards had been placed on the blotter. Her job was to match the postcards to the reports of soldiers who had reached their destination safely. Army procedure required men who were deployed overseas to complete a postcard addressed to their next of kin stating they had successfully travelled to their assigned post. Lists arrived periodically with those soldier's names, and Betty prepared the matched postcards for the outgoing mail. But something extra was on her desk. A blank envelope which obviously held a piece of typing paper. It was sealed.

She looked around, wondering if it was a joke being played on her, but not seeing anyone she opened the envelope. Sitting down in the secretary's chair, she read the typewritten letter.

22 March, 1943

Dear Miss Nugen,

It was very nice making your acquaintance on Saturday. Please excuse Tex's actions, he is very tense. He ships out to England in two weeks and, being a bombardier, is understandably nervous. Also excuse the typewritten letter, my handwriting is not much better than hen scratching, and typing is part of my job.

Do you need to go back into Carlsbad to pick up the photographs from that studio? If you and your friend need a ride, I can get a jeep and escort you into town. Perhaps we all could catch a movie while there. Tex may also want to go, he said he would try.

If this idea is agreeable, please meet me at the bulletin board outside the mess hall at 7:00 pm on Friday evening and we'll make the arrangements for the next day. I hope to see you Friday. If not, whatever will be, will be.

Glenn A. Fields

MSgt Logistics Div.

Betty stared at the letter she found on her desk. She could hear Glenn's smooth baritone voice through the typewritten words on the page. He wanted to see her. Friday and Saturday. And she could almost see "Mrs." in front of the signature. The thought caused a gasp.

"What are you staring at so hard, honey? You look like you saw a ghost!" Ruby perched on the edge of the desk. Startled, Betty looked up and handed over the letter without a word.

Ruby's carefully trimmed eyebrows rose with interest as she read. When finished she let it flutter to the desktop and looked into the distance for a moment. She stood, pulled Betty to her feet and looked into her face. "Well, what are you going to wear on Saturday?"

"Wear? When? What do you mean?"

"I think I'll wear that little flowered number I got in Chattanooga. I'm sure the shoes that go with it are somewhere in my footlocker...haven't needed them for a while."

"You think I-we should go?"

"Think? Heck I know we ought to. That Master Sergeant is sweet on you, dearie." Betty began to protest but Ruby held up her hand. "You didn't see what I saw the other day. Now that Tex, the real Clark, not the Gable lookalike, said he had a lady friend, but I think that was all bluster. He's shipping out soon. Might as well have a little fun!"

"Fun? Oh, Ruby, I don't know…I mean…I can't have fun!"

"And why ever not?"

"Well, I was raised…"

"Baloney. We were all force fed something when we were kids. Now it's up to us to find our own way in the world. Oh, we won't do anything foolish, he's only talking about going to the movie. You've been to the movies before?"

"Of course, but only once with a-a man. And that didn't work out so well. My sister Nancy rescued me from the letch."

"Well, dearie, now ol' Ruby will rescue you if need be, but honestly, I don't see a bit of problem with this plan. Since we're on leave Saturday, we don't have to wear uniforms! You want me to go with you on Friday to meet him?"

"I'm not sure. My mind says it's just a little meeting in front of the mess hall. There'll be lots of people around. But then I think, oh no, I can't."

"Hmm. We'll think on it. At least it will still be daylight. I'd better get to work. Talk to you later." Ruby walked away leaving Betty to sink back into her chair. She folded the letter, pushed it into her pocketbook, and started her day's work.

After lights out, Betty lay on her bunk staring at the ceiling. A glow from the lights outside the barracks revealed cracks and cobwebs not noticed during daylight hours. Around the room, women were drifting off to sleep; the sounds of steady breathing with the occasional snore reminded her of home and of boot camp. Betty was accustomed to sleeping with a crowd. She noticed Ruby's bed squeak a bit as the young women turned onto her side facing Betty's bunk.

"Well," Ruby whispered. "Are you going to meet him?"

Betty remained silent, as a truck rumbled past the barracks. Open windows admitted the dust which coated and permeated everything on the base. Ruby heard Betty draw in a large breath and braced herself for the sneeze that could wake everyone in the barracks. But somehow, Betty stifled it despite the dust. The constant pulverizing of the ground by vehicles and boots created a powder fine haze in the air. And this was only occasionally settled by a light dew falling during an infrequent cool night.

Betty sniffed, rolled to her side and whispered softly. "I hope it's cool enough Saturday to wear those new wool trouser."

"Trousers?" Ruby asked, almost too loudly. She slipped out of her bunk and sat on the edge of Betty's.

"Yes, if they get that jeep again, I think the trousers would be more appropriate for riding that a skirt. Plus..." Betty trailed off.

"Plus, your legs won't show or be available to touch surrounded in Army wool. You have a point. Might as well look the part, they'll probably be in the casual khakis. I guess that little flowered number will have to wait. So you're going to meet him Friday? Want me to tag along?" Ruby reached out toward her friend.

Betty almost laughed, but caught herself. She touched her friend's outreached arm gently. "Of course. I'm sure Tex will be there and he'd be most disappointed if you aren't."

"Hmph. You know, I'm still betting that story about a girlfriend is malarkey."

"Yeah, I imagine inside he's a scared little boy. Understandably."

"That letter said our Texan is shipping out soon. Well, I'll go along with you as body guard...though I think Glenn is a perfect gentleman. That Tex, well, he might need a laugh." Ruby rose and crawled quietly into her own bed.

Betty grinned at her friend's actions. She saw the spark between Tex and Ruby, even if they didn't see it. She also remembered the look in Glenn's eyes, and felt it capable of reaching deep into her soul. Sighing, she closed her eyes to sleep.

The two WAC's walked across the dusty open area between buildings toward the camp bulletin board. As they approached, a small group of soldiers appeared to be gathered near the board. Ruby stopped and put a hand on Betty's forearm.

"I wonder what's going on? Is that music? Well, I mean singing..."

Betty looked at her friend. "Seems to be "Chattanooga ChooChoo."

"Sure does. That's one train and place I don't ever want to see again."

"At least we don't ever have to go back to Ft. Oglethorpe. Though some of that humidity would we welcome in this dusty place," Betty laughed.

The women walked slowly and were surprised at the scene. Glenn and Tex were in the center of the group singing. Tex carried the melody with a strong tenor while Glenn harmonized with deep bass tones. They finished the song with a flourish, receiving a hearty round of applause. Someone requested a slower song, and another called out for "You Are My Sunshine."

As the two men finished the first verse and began the chorus, a rich soprano voice rose above the crowd. The soldiers pulled back, allowing Ruby to enter the center. Her descant harmony blended perfectly with the men as if they had previously rehearsed together. At the end of the song, Ruby hit a high note as Glenn crooned out a low tone. The small crowd clapped and called out their approval.

Just then, a truck rumbled by, scattering the people escaping from the dust cloud. Betty covered her face with one arm and felt the other being pulled toward a building. She could see Ruby hurrying toward an open door. She realized her arm was being gripped by Glenn's large hand, but pulled away to sneeze.

"Oh, my, excuse... AAAHHHHCCCHHHOOOOO!" Glenn caught her as she took a step backward.

"Let's go in the NCO Club and get a bottle of pop," Glenn said after being sure she was all right. The four quickly ducked inside, finding a well lit room with a few empty tables and a small bar. "Four cokes, please, Charlie. And put it on my tab."

Betty looked around nervously. "Are we allowed to be in here?" She moved to stand beside Ruby.

"Honey, don't worry. WAC's come and go from here all the time. I have a view of this building from my office." Ruby placed a protective arm around her friend. "Always wondered what was in here. Looks pretty tame." She threw an elbow into Tex's side. He flinched. "Say, soldier. Won't that girlfriend of yours be insanely jealous since you're here with two WAC's?"

Tex shuffled his feet. "Uh, well…"

"Before we get into Tex's various problems," he turned toward Betty. "First I must ask if you are recovered from that magnificent sneeze. Yes? Good. Does your presence here indicate your consent to join us tomorrow?" A crooked grin belied the serious tone of voice.

Betty hesitated. She glanced at Ruby, then again at Glenn. Seeing the hope and anticipation in his face, she took a breath and ignored Ruby's grin. "Yes, thank you. I must say you describe my sneezes in terms no one has ever used! And, I would like Ruby to come along, as you suggested."

"Well, honey, nobody can sneeze like you can. I'll go if it's all right with Tex, here," Ruby added. "And his lady friend…"

The disconcerted soldier stared at his boots for a moment before glancing up at his friend. Glenn raised an eyebrow and nodded once as if cuing an action.

"Well…if the truth be told, there ain't no girlfriend—"

"Isn't. Isn't a girlfriend," Glenn corrected.

"Isn't. For a farm boy from Missouri, you sure are picky about grammar. Anyway, I made all that up."

"Why?" Betty asked. The man seemed embarrassed.

"Oh, I don't know. With me heading over the pond in a few weeks, and it kind of questionable I could return here in one piece, I just didn't want to get close to anybody..." Tex returned his gaze to his boots.

Ruby glanced and Betty and then returned her gaze to Tex. "It's ok, sweetie. There is a lot to be nervous about. There's a war on, after all. But, in the meantime we can have a few laughs and sing a few songs, can't we?"

Tex turned his eyes to the lovely girl grinning mischievously. "You're really something else, you know it?"

"Why, yes sir, I do..."

"What time should we meet you at the front gate tomorrow?" Betty asked, facing Glenn.

"Front gate? Oh, yes, that'll be fine. Mighty fine! How about 1:00? We can motor into town, pick up your photos, and catch the 3:00 matinee."

Chapter Thirteen

After a nice Saturday afternoon with the guys, and a Sunday picnic the next day, Betty and Ruby spent much of their free time the next week planning Tex's going away party. In an effort to be funny, and to have a good time, Ruby decided on a Hawaiian theme, with grass skirts and hula dancing. Betty was skeptical about dancing the hula, as she had never danced, even at her prom in high school.

But Ruby insisted the effect would be great, since Tex was shipping out to England and would likely not ever see Hawaii like many of the other airmen. Betty agreed, trying to step out of the shell behind which she had hidden for most of her life.

She was pleasantly surprised how comfortable she felt around Glenn. He, being the perfect gentlemen, had done everything possible to make their time together pleasant. Ruby mentioned off handedly a woman in her office had dated briefly dated him and thought he was great, like a big brother. The memory of his hand touching hers in the back seat of the jeep didn't feel brotherly at all.

Returning from town in the back of the jeep that Saturday, he called her attention to a red tailed hawk sitting on a fencepost which flew right over the jeep as they passed. He noticed natural things, like she did. Sitting at her desk, Betty closed her eyes and hoped she wasn't wearing her heart on her sleeve. Ruby certainly wasn't. Tex tried every day for a week to see her, without much success.

Tex seemed to have fallen head over heels for Ruby, but she kept up a barrier, knowing he was going into combat soon. The young man from San Antonio, Texas was quite entertaining. They, along with Glenn, sang songs all the way back from Carlsbad after the Technicolor musical, "Hello Frisco, Hello."

117

Betty was too embarrassed to join in the singing as she had never had a strong voice. But she loved the sound of their voices blended together. The mood was light until Tex mentioned his deploy date in ten days. This was the reason Ruby and Betty concocted the luau party for him.

Following Ruby's example, Betty rolled up her overly large khaki trousers to above her knee, and wrapped the grass skirt around her waist. Ruby had fashioned bandeaus from pillow cases to serve as their tops. The girls tucked bra straps into the bra cups and tied the pillow cases around their chests.

"This is pretty skimpy. I'm not sure about—

Ruby tightened the knot, securing the pillow case in place. "We'll only have these on for a little while, and just for the guys."

"Well, I can't wait to get back into real clothes. I feel like a..." Betty felt the outfit was quite risqué.

"What? A floozy? Nuts, it's just for fun. Stay with me and give it a try."

Other people were bringing the food, but with her usual luck, Ruby acquired three pineapples to decorate the table. They were too green to eat but made festive centerpieces. Several people were coming by later, but the hula dance was to be seen only by Tex and Glenn.

"It would look a lot better if we took off these bulky trousers," Ruby complained. She patted the grass skirt around her legs.

"There is no way under heaven I'm taking off any more than I've already taken off!" Betty was outraged. "Ruby! We can't go out like this!"

"I guess you're right. Wouldn't befit our ladylike reputation, would it? Ok, let's practice a little. I'll hum and you follow my movements. Oh, wait, I almost forgot this…" Ruby reached into a large sack and pulled out an outlandish, fruit and flower covered hat. She moved to put it on Betty.

"Oh, no, you don't. Not on my head!"

"Fine. Then I'll wear it. Pin it in for me, will you?"

With the hat in place with several bobby pins, Ruby hummed the tune she had heard in a movie. She smoothly moved her arms in a flowing motion and rolled her hips side-to-side. Betty copied the actions as best that she could and before long the two were hysterically laughing.

They hurried to the area where the picnic would take place and danced the hula before several sets of widened eyes. When finished, and more importantly before more people arrived, they shuffled back behind the building to put on shirts and roll their pant legs back down. Slipping into shoes, they rejoined group which had brought sandwiches and drinks.

Glenn led a toast to Tex, speaking of friendship, danger, and duty. Just as a resounding version of "He's a Jolly Good Fellow" completed, a flash of lightning crackled, followed immediately by a loud clap of thunder. With only that warning, clouds blew in from the south and began dumping rain on the camp. People scattered in all directions taking cover from the downpour. Ducking under an overhanging roof, Glenn pulled Betty along while he pushed Tex and Ruby under the shelter.

Betty took a breath to relax and realized the sound of the rain on the metal roof above their heads reminded her of the cabin in West Virginia. She looked upward and noticed Glenn, too, looking at the roof. Without looking directly at her, his hand found hers and she felt his strength and character in the grasp.

First looking at the water droplets creating a small stream along the drip line of the roof, Betty braved a glance upward into the six foot tall man's face. One glance into his bright blue eyes was enough. She felt his gaze wrap around her heart and knew, at that moment, she was in love.

Feeling somewhat dizzy, Betty returned her eyes to the ground. Glenn felt her tremble and drew her into his arms. He lowered his face into her hair as she breathed him into her soul. They remained in the embrace even after the shower passed, unaware of Ruby and Tex walking away to clear the sodden sandwiches.

Glenn and Betty realized they had found a comfortable place neither of them had ever known—in the loving arms of each other. She was in the strong embrace of a man she loved and he was holding the woman he would cherish for the rest of his life.

Several weeks after the party and Tex's departure on a Douglas C54 Sky Master beginning his long journey to England, Betty was working at her desk on the post cards to be sent to family when she saw a familiar name as addressee. Ruby hid her feelings, but Betty knew she cried many tears over Tex's leaving.

She remembered the airman clutching a piece of paper in his hand as he held Ruby closely. Later Betty found out Ruby's parents' address and phone number was on that paper. Interestingly, now it appeared Tex put Ruby's name and base address for the post card to be sent. She tucked in her pocketbook to surprise her friend at chow.

Betty found Ruby near the mail call window and presented the postcard with a flourish. Ruby looked at the card and jumped up, off her feet, whooped and came down with her arms around Betty in a big hug. The two women twirled around in a circle expressing their joy. They laughed so loudly Betty almost missed hearing her name called by the mail steward. Ruby released her friend and the clerk handed over two letters addressed to Betty.

The young woman looked at the envelopes with a suddenly furrowed brow. One was from her sister Nancy and the other from her mother. Both were postmarked in Fayetteville on the same day. Glancing at Ruby's still smiling face, she held up the letters. Her friend stopped her joyous dance and guided Betty to a nearby bench.

"Something is wrong. These can't be good news." Betty gazed at the envelopes, weighing each one in her hands. She placed the letter from her mother on the bench between her and Ruby and opened the other.

Dear Sis,

It is with a heavy heart I write this letter to describe the terrible thing that happened recently. A tragedy has occurred to our dear nephew, Les. He was grievously injured in an accident. He lost his left arm and eye—yes, his good eye.

The boys were at the deep part of the creek aiming to catch some fish the easy way. Impatience and mischievousness led to the accident. Les was to throw a stick of dynamite into the water to stun the fish. Fred had a net to scoop them up. Don manned the battery and wires to detonate the explosive. However, the wires somehow slipped from Don's hands and fell directly onto the battery making the connection before Les threw the stick of dynamite. It exploded in his hand, taking his left arm off at the elbow and the concussion shattered some bones in his face and ruptured his left eye.

The sound of the dynamite followed by the boys' screaming was heard at Fanny's house. Paul was there, getting some eggs for his wife and little boy. He ran to help, scooped the bloody and fainting Les up in his arms and carried him to the car. After putting a tourniquet of sorts on Les' arm, Fanny made sure the other boys were all right and rode with them to the Oak Hill hospital.

Thankfully, Katherine was on duty and she calmly took charge and cared for our nephew. I'm glad I didn't hear about it until after he was all bandaged up, all that blood might have made me faint! Yes, I've gotten that tender footed. But it is so sad. Losing his good eye. The left one has always been crossed. But Katherine said the eye doctor who cleaned up the ruptured eye ball took a look at the right eye and said it could be straightened out some with surgery, and he could do it. That gives us hope he will be able to see and read and write again and the money mama has been saving should help pay for it.

So, we are all saving our pennies to help pay for his hospital bills and get him that eye surgery. He is still in the hospital, but Katherine plans to take him home to stay in her guest room so he can be well cared for and kept quiet. She can change the bandages and take him to follow up visits. She is truly a good soul. I am so glad she is part of our family.

That's all I have for now. Send what money you can to help. Take care and I am sending all my love.

Love from your sister

Nancy

Betty stared at Nancy's signature as a tear escaped her eye. She seemed transfixed until Ruby touched her arm. "What is it?" she asked.

Betty passed the letter to her friend to read while she opened the other envelope. Breathing deeply, she looked at her mother's handwriting. It seemed shaky and uneven, somehow frail or even uncertain. But the words were strong and to the point.

Dear Betty Irene,

Another trial and tribulation has been laid upon our family. Fanny's boys were playing with some dynamite and somehow it blew up, ripping Les's arm off and it put out his good eye. Katherine is looking after him since you are gone and the others are all busy. If you were here, I would bring him home to care for. But he is going to be all right, God willing.

What you can do is send more money home.
There will be many doctor bills and, him being your
nephew, I'm sure you would want to do the Godly
thing and help out. This will pass, but the Lord will
provide.

I trust you are doing well out there in the desert.
We do look forward to your letters and are proud
you are serving our country in these trying times. I
pray every day for your and your brothers' safety in
those foreign lands. The hope is it is God's will to
bring all of you safely home.

God Bless,

Mother

Betty stared straight ahead, barely feeling Ruby take the
paper from her hands. Those hands began to shake, causing her
to clasp them tightly and hold them in her lap. Her whole body
began to tremble. Ruby place her arm around Betty's shoulders
and felt her wilt a bit. Betty unclasped her hand, placed them on
her thighs and breathed deeply. At last she sighed.

"What are you going to do?" Ruby asked.

"I guess I should send all my pay home. I don't really need
much money here."

"That's true. Ruby removed her arm and leaned backward
with a mischievous grin. "Since you don't drink and don't
smoke, you are pretty low maintenance. Besides, you have that
steady beau to foot the bill if you go out somewhere."

Betty's head jerked upward to protest that statement. But just then, a grinning Glenn walked toward the women. Before she thought what she was doing, Betty ran to him and burst into tears. He wrapped his arms around her and looked over her head toward Ruby with a question in his eyes. The woman shrugged her shoulders and held up the letter. Betty pulled away and dried her eyes. The pair settled on the bench beside Ruby and Betty folded the letters neatly and tucked them into their envelopes. He listened carefully as she explained what had caused her to become so upset.

"How terrible," he said when she finished the story. Glenn shook his head side-to-side. "Isn't that the nephew you said had a good head for figures?"

"Yes, it is. He's as sharp as a whip when it comes to arithmetic. Now he can't see. How will he be able to learn at school? I'll have to send them money. But, a girl does need some things…"

"Oh, you'd be surprised at what all they have over at the supply shack. I saw the inventory list. All kinds of stuff. Why, they've even got those WAC beauty kits we saw in the paper back in Oglethorpe. Remember?"

"Yes, the newspaper made such a big deal out of that shaving kit looking thing with a little powder and lipstick. It was downright embarrassing."

"Right, but if they're giving them away, I'll take one! Come on, let's go shopping on Uncle Sam's nickel. But you keep some of that paycheck. It's a good thing to have a little jingle in your pocket." She picked up the post card. "Oh, lookee here, Glenn! Tex made it to jolly old England in one piece."

Glenn stood. "Good! That's good news. Now all we have to hope for is that he can come home in one piece. You girls go on, I'll catch up with you after chow. I've been called to a meeting so I gotta go now. Betty, you'll be all right. Everything will be all right."

Betty looked up at the dark haired man and saw truth and honesty in his eyes. Breathing in, she rose and placed her hand on his chest, feeling his heartbeat. His hand covered hers and they drew closer together. Ruby noticed a WAC officer walking in their direction. She rose and grabbed her friend's elbow.

"Oh, you two, quit that. Come on!" She pulled her friend away just as the older woman came around the corner of the building. The women and Glenn casually went their separate ways.

"Uh, oh. AAAHHHHCCCHHHOOOOO!"

"Good timing, honey. That should convince that officer there wasn't any public display of affection going on here..." Betty and Ruby hurried away

Chapter Fourteen

As the weeks passed, Glenn and Betty grew closer, often they enjoyed just sitting in the grass near one of the many buildings on the base. Comfortable in each other's company, each knew this was love. But Glenn feared the rumor of men in his group being shipped out to Guam might interrupt their romance. They sat in the shadow of a vehicle; Betty leaned against the front tire of a vehicle while Glenn reclined nearby. Their quiet time was interrupted as Ruby came running toward them.

"Betty! Betty! Glenn! Oh, Betty.!"

The two quickly rose to their feet to see why Ruby was so distraught. She shoved a telegram at Glenn and fell into her friend's embrace.

"A telegram? It's from Tex?" He paused before reading it aloud. "ARRIVED AT VET HOSPITAL NEW YORK STOP TOOK A SHELL IN ARM OVER GERMANY MIGHT LOSE IT STOP ALMOST MADE 25 STOP DOING OKAY SO FAR STOP AMMO BELT SAVED LIFE STOP"

"Lose his arm? Ammo belt? Oh my goodness!" Betty cried.

"Seems like I've heard of those belts of shells the gunners wear stopping bullets from hitting their bodies. He must have had to man one of the guns. The flak jackets might work for flak, but those big rounds the enemy fighters fire will go right through them."

"Imagine, a bullet stopping a bullet. Wait, he doesn't have any family, does he?" Betty asked.

"No. He was adopted and even those parents kicked him out when he was a kid. Poor guy. I've got to request leave and somehow get to New York."

127

"Hold on there. How can you be sure he'll still be there?" Glenn asked. "Wait, I take back that question. You'll go anyway and find the poor sap. I'll check, but I'm pretty sure there's a transport returning to the east coast day after tomorrow. Maybe you could hitch a ride."

"That would be wonderful, thanks." Ruby straightened her uniform and dried her eyes. "Whew, I needed to get that out. Come with me to see the CO, will you, honey?" she asked of her friend. Betty nodded, touched Glenn on the forearm and the two women left him standing next to the car which had so briefly shielded them from the war.

Two weeks later, Betty finished her week's work and left her office around 5:30 on Friday. She and Glenn had a date to go into Carlsbad to see a movie, so she planned to make a quick stop by mail call and then go freshen up for her evening out.

She retrieved two letters from the window, one from her sister Nancy and the other from Ruby in New York. She opened it while walking toward the barracks. It was just a short note stating Tex was doing well and his arm was saved. She would catch a plane back to Carlsbad as soon as she could get one. "I might even beat this letter there!" She wrote.

Betty grinned and tucked the letter in her pocket, as she entered the barracks. Hoping for good news about Les, she opened Nancy's letter after sitting on the green, wool blanket spread neatly across her bunk. She kicked off her shoes and pulled off the thick socks and thought of walking barefoot in the grass at home.

Dear Sis,

Now something else bad has happened. Oh, Les is doing pretty well, but I don't know how to describe this—Paul is missing! Last Thursday he took some car parts to Alice for one of her taxis and never came back home. No one has seen his car, and his little boy just sits at the front window of their home waiting for daddy to come home. He just vanished. Something very bad must have occurred, he wouldn't just leave like that on purpose. He loves that boy and his wife! We are all worried sick about it. How could this happen?

Mother is distraught about it. He is her baby boy. It seems rather ironic that he went to war, was injured in England and came home to recuperate, only to have something like this happen right here at home! This not knowing is pure torture.

Fanny is holding up well considering all the problems with Les' injuries. The boys are feeling so guilty about it all. Things are moving well, thanks to your generous help. We put a down payment on the surgeon to straighten out his lazy eye. Mother asked me to thank you specifically. I know Les is a favorite nephew of yours and we all want the best for him. Katherine has been a huge help. She knows what she's doing when it comes to nursing...well and just about everything else, too.

On a much brighter note, I was thrilled to read in your letter about your life out there in the women's army. And that you met a great man. That Glenn sounds like a real dream boat inside and out. I knew you leaving West Virginia was the right thing to do.

After things settle down, I'm thinking of moving to Columbus Ohio myself.

Gotta run. Pray for Paul's safe return and let's hope he can come home soon.

Love, your sis

Nancy

Stunned, Betty allowed the letter to slip from her hand and drift to the floor where it settled under her bunk. Paul was missing? She had been told in one of Nancy's letters after he was injured in England, he was transferred to a desk job in Virginia. He drove home every weekend to see his wife and child. Nancy's letter was dated March 10, 1944 so over three weeks had passed since Paul disappeared. Surely he was home?

Betty decided it was time to try out the new pay phone just outside the base front gate. Soldiers and visitors were often seen in the booth, talking into the receiver, but she had never used it. Quickly pulling on her socks and shoes, she picked up the letter, her change purse and address book and hurried out of the barracks. She walked purposefully across the dusty ground toward the front gate.

"Hey, toots! Where you headed in such a hurry?" A soldier called as Betty passed by some offices. She ignored the question, per her training and general revulsion for the ogling eyes of men.

"That's Glenn Fields' girl, better keep quiet," another man offered.

Betty grinned slightly. She never dreamed she would be called something like Glenn's "girl." She kept on walking, not letting anyone distract her from the mission. However, Glenn was leaving his office. Hearing his own name called, he hurried out to see what was going on. He saw Betty walking with purpose toward the front gate and unashamedly ran to catch up with her.

Two days after a futile phone call, with Glenn's assistance, to Alice in West Virginia—there was no news about Paul—Ruby arrived with Tex in tow. His arm had improved so much the brass sent him back to Carlsbad to train new bombardiers. The Navy and Marines achieved victory after victory in the Pacific and the Army Engineers were constructing airfields almost as quickly as the islands were taken.

He told of his time in the bomber over Germany. Betty and Ruby were transfixed as he spoke. The haunted and faraway look in his normally twinkling eyes spoke of the horrors he had endured.

"One mission, the flak was heavy. I mean beating holes in that B-29 as easy as a poking a hot knife through butter. Felt like sitting in a tin can, waiting for the guy target practicing to find my part of the can. It was such a helpless feeling, nothing we could do except ride it out.

"Then, when the flak stopped, those Messerschmitt fighters showed up. Thank God for the Mustangs. Oh how I would have loved to be a pilot of one of those sleek babies, out there shooting back at the guy trying to kill my friends. Some of those pilots were cocky on the ground, but, buddy, they could fly those planes and saved our butts more than once.

"Course getting hurt cut my time short there, but I have to say, I'm not a bit sorry about leaving. So many boys, so many planes, they never made it back to England. On that mission where I caught that shell, the tail gunner was killed as one of those Germans strafed the back of our aircraft.

We limped back on two engines and had two dozen holes of various sizes in the fuselage and tail. That poor guy, the tail gunner, he was from Louisiana, you know, a Cajun. Fun fellow. Boy could he laugh. Bullets about cut him in half. Yep, leave me here in the desert. I think I'll stay on US soil for the rest of my life!"

"We sometimes forget the horror of war." Glenn clapped his friend on his good shoulder. "I guess we have to find a place in our hearts to bury that horror and try to bring out good."

Betty and Ruby grinned with appreciation of Glenn's words. Ruby put her arms around Tex's neck and gave him a big kiss on the lips. Betty pushed her arm through Glenn's and they walked away from the shroud of sadness remaining from Tex's story of war.

The two couples fell into an easy routine. By the summer of 1944, Guam, a United States territory which had been invaded and seized by Japan on December 8, 1941, one day after Pearl Harbor was attacked had liberated by Marines. Regaining Guam was a huge victory for the United States in means of morale and reestablishing a secure air base within reach of mainland Japan. Rumors began flying of Army Air Corps support personnel being transferred to places throughout the Pacific to help supply the advancing war effort. Those rumors persisted for months.

On a cool Saturday evening in October 1944, Glenn and Betty were walking hand in hand through Carlsbad. All the shops and offices were closed and only a few military people were about in town. He stopped at the end of a sidewalk and pulled her into his arms. Breathing into her hair, he softly said,

"It's looking like the orders to ship out to the Pacific will come in after the first of the year, honey."

Betty pulled back and looked up into his face. His eyes softened and he took a deep breath.

"What do you say about us getting married before I have to go?"

She buried her face into his chest and wrapped her arms around his waist. Nodding, she whispered, "Yes!"

"Yes? Really?" Glenn looked into the sky and let out a whoop. Betty laughed.

"Yes! I'll marry you! But we'll have to ask Mama. We'll write a letter. Oh, where will we live? I mean after the war. Our homes are so far apart."

"Easy now. Certainly I'll write to your mother, and ask for your hand in marriage properly. As far as where we'll live, my oldest brother has a line on some property in Dallas, Texas he thinks I can get for a homestead. I can build things, had all that training in the CCC, you know. We'll live in Texas. Hey, we should get married in Texas!"

"Texas? Tex is from Texas, isn't he?"

"Indeed he is. I've already spoken to him. He knows a justice of the peace who can do the ceremony. Of course, no details are nailed down yet...there is a war on, you know..."

"Oh, surely this war will be over soon!"

"I don't know. The Japanese will fight to the last man. We have to get closer to beat them. That's where Guam comes in."

"But with you overseas..."

"Aw, everything will be fine. Hurrah! We're going to get married!" he shouted to the world.

Some of the people around shouted congratulations at the obvious good news. Glenn picked Betty up and twirled her around. Their joy sparkled. Putting her down, he grabbed her hand and they hurried to the jeep.

Back at the base, Betty could barely hold in her news, but they didn't dare tell anyone until they heard back from her mother. The base had a few apartments for married people. After sending the letter to Betty's mother to formerly ask her blessing upon the marriage, Glenn planned to discretely determine if one was available before they announced the news.

Weeks passed, but the return answer finally came with well wishes from all the family in West Virginia. Things were looking good for the happy couple.

Chapter Fifteen

After an overnight train trip to San Antonio, Texas, Glenn and Betty stood in front of a Bexar County Justice of the Peace. No rings were exchanged, no rice tossed, and no bouquet was thrown, but there was a maid of honor and best man. The happy couple was married and had a Texas marriage certificate to prove it. Tex took everyone, including the judge and his wife, to a fancy steak house to celebrate. The couples spent a few days touring the missions and Alamo before returning to Carlsbad.

On their last weekend before Glenn was to ship out to Guam, the couple saw the inspiring and extremely patriotic film "This is The Army" with Ronald Reagan and Jane Wyman. That same Saturday afternoon in late February, Betty asked to walk on the sunny side of the street. When they approached Angelo's photography studio, she paused at the door. The sun reflected off the windows, glaring in Glenn's eyes.

"Let's go in here for a minute, I have to pick up something." Betty said while pulling Glenn's arm. He allowed her to coerce him into the building all the while fighting an urge to laugh aloud. Not at Betty, at himself. He couldn't quite believe his luck in finding a girl like Betty.

Inside, Angelo exclaimed when he saw her and quickly pulled a large envelope from behind his counter. Gushing over the newlyweds, he mumbled something about a wasted opportunity to be a wedding photographer, as he hurried from the room. After he left, Glenn thought he heard laughter, but was distracted by Betty.

"This is a gift for you, dear. To take with you…when…to put in your knapsack," she said quietly.

He looked on the counter and saw a photograph of his new bride. It was a small, wallet sized image of Betty in her WAC uniform. Angelo had colorized it to show her blushing cheeks and red lips. Glenn glanced at his bride and saw the same image standing beside him.

Betty then pulled a hard backed book from the brown sack. Glenn looked closely at the title, "A Book of Thoughts and Quotes," he read aloud. It appeared to be quite old. He opened the cover and saw a name printed neatly on the first page. Looking further, he noticed the book had been printed in 1916, the year of his birth. His eyes widened as Betty explained.

"I found it in the second hand store on the edge of town. It belonged to a B-29 co-pilot who went down over Germany and had no family. His buddies sold his belongings to order a marker in the man's hometown. I thought a deep thinker like you might like a book like this...especially since it was previously owned by a lost airman."

Glenn put a hand on hers and squeezed it gently. Then he looked at the name written on the page. Noticing a pen lying on the counter, he took it up and scrawled his own name just below the other.

She reached over to turn pages to a place she marked. The book opened to reveal a five by seven photograph of Betty in the flight jacket, her hair somewhat disheveled and eyes looking toward something unknown. But he knew what she had been looking at that day.

"That day." His deep voices echoed his thoughts. That's when I saw you through that very window right over there. He took the picture right when—"

"Right when I saw you for the first time, my Clark Gable. Only so much better, because you are real. Put this picture in your wallet and carry it with you. And don't end up ditched in the ocean, or smothered by a boa constrictor, or some such horror."

"Madame, I will do my very best. Once we get there, there shouldn't be much danger. From what I understand, between the Japanese and American bombing, there's not a beach, or a tree left on the island, much less any large snakes." He noticed a passage had been circled in pen.

"Marriage is the most natural state of man, and... the state in which you will find solid happiness," he read aloud. "Old Ben Franklin said that, eh? Well, I imagine the feller was right!"

Glenn took his wife into his arms and kissed her firmly. From the back room, Angelo could be heard snickering with delight. Releasing her, Glenn picked up the photograph and held it next to her face. Calling to the photographer, he said, "Well done, my man. It's a keeper. And so is she!"

Three days later at the break of dawn, Ruby, Betty and Tex stood beside the air strip as a Curtiss-Douglas C-46 transport aircraft taxied past. It turned into the wind, gained speed and left the New Mexico semi-arid desert with a goal of reaching San Diego, California for refueling. It would then go on to Hawaii, and finally cross the wide Pacific to Guam. Betty could picture Glenn, huddled in the fuselage along with thirty other men, getting as comfortable as possible. Shivering and feeling ill, she grabbed Ruby's arm and started to faint. Tex caught her in time to ease her limp body onto the ground.

Immediately awaking, Betty was dismayed at finding herself on the grass. Ruby chaffed her wrists while Tex called for help.

Refusing to stay on the ground, Betty struggled to her feet and waived off the field medic who was rushing toward them.

"I'm fine. Never mind me. I'm all right. Ruby—I think we'd better get back to the barracks. I do feel a bit—drained."

"Sure thing, honey. Just hang on to me. I guess it's a good thing you didn't completely move out of our fancy abode. We'll see you later, Tex!" Ruby called out before lowering her voice. "You sure you're ok? I mean you're as white as a sheet."

"Yes, yes, it's just all the excitement and nervousness, I'm sure. But I do feel like I need to lie down for a while."

"I know how you feel. When Tex took off that time to go to the fighting, I thought I'd lose my lunch. Maybe we should get you something to eat."

Betty shuddered. "No! I mean, no, I couldn't—just help me get to my bunk in private without every Tom, Dick and Harry sticking their spoon in my bowl of soup."

"Ha! Haven't heard that one before. Yep, tough ol' broad, ain't you, there, farm girl? Sure, sure. Let's go." Ruby laughed aloud, happy to see Betty's spunk reappear.

Betty lay on the woolen blanket feeling the same queasiness she had felt for about a week. Wondering if she could be pregnant, she debated with herself what to do. If the Army found out she was with child they would discharge her immediately. Betty shook off the worrisome thought with the intent to continue doing her job, going about the daily routine as normal.

However, she wondered if she could terminate her enlistment and leave the Army before anyone would know. Even Ruby, she decided, would not be told for a while. She couldn't even write to Nancy to tell her the news, as the Army censored every letter in and out of the base.

She sat up on the bunk and spied a newspaper on Ruby's footlocker. A front page article caught her eye. Picking it up, she read in disbelief how 2500 women mobbed a Chicago, Illinois department store for a chance at one of 1500 alarm clocks which had just been delivered. The article went on to say those clocks had not been available in over two years due to the demands on raw materials for the war effort. Happy for the distraction, Betty giggled aloud and didn't hear someone approaching.

"Yeah, isn't that something?" Ruby saw Betty reading the article and plopped onto the bunk beside her. "I declare never again in my life will I need an alarm clock. Plus, after the war is over, I hope to never, ever hear Reveille."

Before he left, Glenn left an envelope of papers with Betty showing the purchase of three acres on the southern edge of Dallas, Texas. His older brother had already set up housekeeping there with his wife, two sons and one daughter. Betty remembered the eldest son was in the regular Army and on a ship bound for England.

Being the youngest of a large family, Glenn's nephews were only about ten years his junior. This was another point on which he and Betty connected, as she had the same situation in her family. There was nothing for them in Missouri, so the brothers scattered all over the western United States in search of their own destinies. Betty realized the same went for her, so starting over in Texas was as good a choice as any. She thought of the climate of Carlsbad and imagined Dallas was close to the same...except for less snow in the winter.

"Let's go outside. Tex is—"

The roar of a four engine aircraft flying too low stopped Ruby from finishing her sentence. The women rushed out of the barracks. Betty, Ruby, and looked into the sky to see a B-29 with only part of its landing gear down. The plane rumbled away, apparently circling the base.

"Oh my God! There was a plane in England that couldn't put down the landing gear. Hydraulics were shot up or something. If these guys have had a hydraulic failure, they're in trouble."

"Don't they have another way to put the gear down?" Betty voice tightened.

"Sure. If you have four or five guys to crank them down manually. And it's a slow go. Plus, we train with only the pilot, copilot, bombardier trainer and trainee. That leaves only two guys to man the cranks. Unless the copilot isn't high and mighty and pitches in."

"Look! The emergency vehicles are headed out there!" Ruby exclaimed.

"Let's go!" Tex cried, grabbing both women by the hand and pulling them along. They ran toward the air strip and joined a small crowd of soldiers and WAC's. The plane circled several times. Word spread through the onlookers he was running out of fuel.

"They'll be lucky to get down," someone in the crowd said gravely.

"It'll be a belly landing, hope they don't catch fire," another said.

"The gear, it's not in place!"

"Look! He's coming in! Watch out!"

Betty pulled back from the crowd and said a quick prayer for the crew. As the aircraft approached the field, the pilot fought to keep level flight and seemed to be aiming for the dirt area on the far side of the landing strip. He eased the huge aircraft down to earth and disappeared into a dust storm created by the propellers and the fuselage plowing up the New Mexico desert. The B-29 slid for hundreds of yards before coming to a stop. When the dust cleared, fire was apparent.

"Oh, no. It's on fire! Those guys, they gotta get outta there!" Tex exclaimed. He took a few steps forward but knew to stop and let the trained personnel respond.

"There's one! He jumped! Where's the others?" Another voice from the crowd asked.

"This is horrible, will they be all right? Can they get out?" Ruby asked, tugging on Tex.

Through the dust and smoke, a jeep hurried toward the base hospital. Three men waved to the crowd, but one lay prone on the back of the vehicle. The crowd of people followed the jeep, anxious to check on the crew. Betty stayed back, watching the aircraft burn and thinking of her brothers in the war. And especially of Paul, who was lost so close to home.

The thought occurred to her that him being missing in West Virginia was as bad as if he was reported "Missing in Action" in Europe. This was the reality of war. Men injured, often even killed. Airplanes on the ground in ruins—not flying proudly through the sky. She straightened her back, proud to be in the uniform, proud to be a part of the fight. Those other countries started something the United States would have to finish. Betty knew in her heart her country would triumph over the trials of war—and was glad she could help.

A few days later, Betty sat at her desk with widened eyes. With one hand pressed against her stomach and the other bracing against the desk, she felt the bile rise in her throat. Rising, she hurried to the ladies room outside the building and was sick. After vomiting everything she had eaten, she leaned against the wall and breathed deeply to regain her strength.

This was the third time in a week she had been sick in the morning. Sliding down to crouch near the concrete floor, she felt a wave of awareness come over her body and soul. Betty remembered her sisters complaining of morning sickness early in their pregnancies. Suddenly, she realized her menstrual cycle hadn't occurred in two months. Betty was sure she was going to have a baby.

Chapter Sixteen

Throughout the day, Betty kept to herself, even begging off lunch with Ruby in the chow hall. Afraid to eat, she remained riveted to her desk. By late afternoon, her stomach complained with hunger pangs. She had to make a decision. Several decisions. At quitting time, she hurried to Ruby's work area.

"Oh good, you're still here! Let's go to dinner, I'm starving!" She said brightly.

Ruby stepped back to look at her friend. "Really? You've been acting strange lately, and were close to rude to me at lunch, you know."

"I know. I'm sorry." She linked arms with the confused woman. They walked out of the building, where Betty stopped short of the dirt street area. "Ruby, I've got to tell you something."

"What? Why the mystery?"

"Well, it could be that I'm…well, I think I'm…" Betty trailed off, unable to say the words aloud. She sighed.

"Goodness gracious sakes alive! You're going to have a baby?"

Betty grabbed her friend's arm. "Shhh, not so loud. I've got to keep this a secret for a while—well, until I'm sure. What should I do? My sisters all had babies, I know how that part happens, but how do you know you're going to…"

"This is something you want, right? Even with Glenn overseas?"

"Oh, yes, with all my heart. I want to have my own family!"

143

"Okay, then, we'd best go ahead and make a doctor appointment in town. They'll discharge you anyway if it's positive. What if this is a false alarm?"

Betty considered for a moment. "If I'm not…with child… I'll stay in the WAC. There no choice. On the other hand, if it is…positive…it's the same thing. Going home to have the baby is the only thing I can do."

"All right, toots. Truth is, I have a doctor appointment in town tomorrow for the same problem. Tex said he'd take me, no reason you can't come along for the ride."

"What? Oh, Ruby. Is it…did you and Tex…?"

"How else would it happen? Betty, dear, you know I'm no angel. But Tex and I love each other. That's the other thing we're going to do in town tomorrow. Get married. Then everything is AOK."

"Well, it's for the best, I'm sure. My goodness, this is a turn of events, isn't it?"

"And one good thing will be to get us out of this desert before summertime!" Ruby declared. Betty nodded.

"And before spring, when the hay fever starts up. Speaking of… AAAHHHHCCCHHHOOOOO!"

"Lord, yes. We want to avoid you sneezing at all costs…" Ruby winked at her friend. "Let's go to supper. I'm starving for some reason."

"Me, too. Oh, maybe it's true what they say about eating for two!"

The next day, both women were told they were "in the family way" and Betty stood for Ruby in front of the Justice of the Peace in Carlsbad. Each woman took the letter from the doctor's office to the WAC commanding officer to tender their resignation due to pregnancy.

Members of the WAC were aware they would be discharged without fanfare and sent back to their homes six months after the war ended. Many felt they should have the option to continue a military career. But there were barriers. The Army commanding officers declared the WAC was of great importance and vital to the military effort. However, those same leaders tolerated gossip, discrimination, and otherwise harmful actions from men in the Air Corps toward the women serving in the same service.

This reality made the decision to leave easier, despite the necessity as a result of their condition. At the end of March 1944, the two women lowered themselves into a staff car which would take them to the train station in Carlsbad. Their unit formed up in salute, standing at attention until the car exited the front gate. Many of the women had been sorry to see them leave, but were happy for them, as well. At the commanding officer's signal, the group turned as one and marched back to their section of the base. Men stared, some in admiration, some with derision. None, however, said a word. There was no denying the obvious pride and competence of the WAC unit.

On the bus, Ruby stretched her legs out in front admiring her new sandals. Betty glanced down at the T-strap pumps she wore. Leaving the base in civilian clothes felt very strange to the women. Both had been required to leave their uniforms behind, presumably for other to women to use. Betty considered the face she might not be able to see her feet in the near future. Further, wouldn't want to wear stylish shoes in the log cabin on the mountain. She would pack them safely away, along with the dresses and other things she had purchased to perhaps use later.

No letter had been received from Glenn in Guam to say he knew she had left the WAC, was pregnant, and going home. Betty confirmed twice the Army had her address in Laurel Creek, West Virginia. Her mail should be forwarded. She vowed to write several letters to him while on the train trip east and post them at every possible opportunity. Hostilities in the Pacific made mail service sketchy, but she would make the effort to keep Glenn informed as to where, and what, she was doing.

According to the telegrams she exchanged with Nancy, her family was excited to know she was coming home. The mystery of Paul's disappearance still hung over them, but several of the brothers had returned home from Europe, injured or finished with their tours of duty. Les was doing well, excelling in his studies, just as expected. She hoped her contributions to his surgeries helped put him in a position to do well in school. If he could overcome the physical limitations, she knew his exceptional mind would take him to intellectual levels no Nugen had ever gone.

In Carlsbad, Ruby and Tex said a tearful goodbye, and Betty also received a strong embrace from the big man. He promised to write, or even call on the phone, if he was to be transferred. There was talk throughout the service about something big happening in Europe, and he expected to be sent to England at any time. The two women boarded a passenger train and settled in for the long trip to Saint Louis.

At every stop, the two women escaped from the smoky train car to get fresh air, be sick or hit the newsstand. On one leg of the trip a man in a nearby seat smoking a cheap cigar caused Ruby to run to the ladies room to vomit. On another leg, Betty sneezed and sneezed until, to Ruby's delight, the woman wearing too much perfume sitting in front of them moved away and didn't come back. At some of the train stations, Ruby stocked up on newspapers to read. Betty bought a journal, to write down her memories and thoughts along the way. She would read the papers, also, to keep up with the war in the Pacific.

In one of those papers, Ruby noticed a photograph. The caption described a waist gunner in a B-29 Superfortress receiving a blood transfusion right there in the airplane. Betty found the idea close to preposterous. But the idea of a mobile blood supply got Ruby to thinking.

"I wonder if, after the war, there will be a big supply of surplus vehicles. I could take one of the nicer trucks, fix it up, paint it real pretty, and put the equipment in to take blood donations. Hey, maybe I could contract with a hospital, they could pay my expenses, and I drive around with a nurse type person doing blood drives."

"You think there will be a need, after the war, I mean?"

"With all those GI's coming home, driving cars across the country, I bet there'll be a need for blood transfusions due to automobile accidents alone. Never mind surgeries and who knows what the doctors will come up with. Hmm, I'll have to think on that."

"It's a good idea in a city like where you live. Not in the Appalachians, though."

"True, though you'll live in a city before it's all done, I bet."

"Three acres outside Dallas is not the 'city.' But when we change trains in Dallas, I guess I'd better get out and look around!"

When the train pulled into Dallas, Texas, the women collected their bags and began walking across the station. Betty caught a whiff of something, stopped and sneezed so loudly, several people turned and looked.

"AAAHHHHCCCHHHOOOOO!"

"Lordy, woman. I hope you don't sneeze like that close to time to have that baby! It'll just come right on out under the pressure!" Ruby laughed.

A woman crossed the terminal with purpose. In her official looking uniform, she appeared quite formidable and people yielded to her progress. As she approached Ruby and Betty, a wide smile appeared on her face.

"Betty! Betty Nugen the WAC!"

"Delores? Oh, my goodness gracious! Ruby, this is the WAVE I met on the way to basic training. Delores, this is my friend Ruby. We've been friends since boot camp. How did you find me in this crowd?" Betty accepted a big hug from the uniformed woman.

"Are you kidding? Is there anyone else in this whole wide world who sneezes like you do?" She laughed. "Pleased to meet you, Ruby. So, why no uniforms? Where are you headed?"

As the women caught up on the news with each other, they realized they would be on the same train to Saint Louis. Delores was travelling to Washington D.C. to help with the christening of several new warships. She was delighted to meet up with the two former WAC's and convinced the purser to allow them to sit together despite the separate seat assignments.

Not unexpectedly, an excessive amount of perfume on a nearby passenger triggered Betty to produce several window

148

rattling sneezes. This caused the wearer of said perfume to make a scene. Delores suggested they get a glass of tea, Betty agreed, and Ruby had a parting remark for the lady as they rose from their seats.

"I've heard some folks say perfume stinks purdy. Hmm, sometime it just stinks! Come on girls, let's get some fresh air."

After crossing the Red River into Oklahoma, the three women claimed a table in the dining car, with the plan of holding it for as long as possible. Being mid-afternoon, only a few other people were in the car and several of the windows were open.

"All right. Now we can talk. You know, I've known a few WAVES who married and got pregnant, not necessarily in that order, and left the service."

"I guess it makes a little sense, although there's no reason I couldn't continue to do my job...well until it got too uncomfortable to sit at my desk," Betty said thoughtfully. "This attitude that a woman is so fragile when she's...you know...is silly. If the policy makers could have seen my sister, Fanny, well I declare that woman could have a baby in the morning, bake bread in the afternoon, and kill, pluck and cook a chicken for supper all in one day."

"Maybe you mountain folk are tougher than most of us," Ruby laughed. "Take me to the hospital and knock me completely out when it is my time. Tough I ain't!"

"Don't you have doctors in West Virginia, Betty?" Delores asked.

"Of course. Our doctor came up to the farm when one of us was real sick. But it had to be real bad to send for the doctor. Sometimes when he was around Laurel Creek, he would come

149

up the hill to get some eggs and butter in advance payment for services to be rendered. With all the children, it was a good chance we would need something doctored."

"Bartering? With the doctor?" Ruby asked. At Betty's nod she continued. "Well, the ol' doc' wouldn't get very rich that way, would he?"

"Maybe not, but as my mom would say, 'It's all good and fine to have diamonds and money, but you can't eat those things like you can biscuits and honey!'" Delores slapped her thigh. The women laughed aloud.

"Oh, my, you are a stitch, Delores!" Ruby declared. "Say, Betty told me about what your job is in the WAVES, did you ever meet any stars?"

"Not very often, but let me tell you something exciting that happened a few months ago. You've heard of Frank Sinatra?" Delores asked.

"The singer on the radio?" Betty asked

"Yeah, he was on 'The Hit Parade' for a while," Ruby added.

"That's the one. He has the bluest eyes I ever saw. He's going to be real famous someday, I bet. Anyway, I was in San Francisco arranging lodging for the entertainers. My team was to make sure he and his people were well cared for."

"Ooh, hubba, hubba!" Ruby said.

"No, no. Nothing like that!" Delores grinned. "Although, he did invite the whole team, including the Admiral, up to his suite for drinks. My, oh, my that place was plush!"

"Did it have a view of the Golden Gate Bridge? I've always wanted to see that," Ruby asked.

"I don't really know…I was concentrating on what was going on inside the rooms."

"Well, tell us! What happened? Or is it…classified?" Betty teased.

"Okay, Okay, I'll spill the beans. Oh, he was smooth, that one. Even asked me out to dinner and dancing for the next evening." Delores looked at her friend.

"But…you didn't go, did you?" Betty asked with knowing eyes and a grin.

Delores put on a visage of innocence and placed her hand on the table. "Why do you ask that?"

"I'm not sure, but it wouldn't look good, would it? A woman in uniform out on the town with a celebrity and all that comes with that." Betty covered the WAVES' hand with her own.

Ruby almost jumped out of her seat. "You're right! I can see the newspaper headline now…"

"Exactly, my friends!" Delores responded. "The reporters would have a field day. They'd snap a few pictures of us dancing and put them on the front page. The captions would read something like, 'Crooner Swoons over WAVE – Woman Navy NCO cuts rug with Frank Sinatra.' All that ran through my head standing there in the hotel room!"

The women laughed so loudly, the people on the other side of the dining car turned to stare. Calming themselves, they paused while the waiter refilled their tea glasses.

151

"Good gravy. That would have been awful for you and all women in uniform!" Betty said softly. Ruby wasn't so demure.

"Yes! Thank you Delores for not ruining the whole thing for women serving in the armed forces. An incident like that would give Colonel Hobby a heart attack and ruin the possibility for women to be in the service for a generation or two."

Betty nodded agreement. "Yes, indeed. We may not be in the Women's Air Corp anymore, but that shouldn't keep our daughters and granddaughters from being able to serve our country."

"Maybe so, but I'd be sure to warn her about some of the more unpleasant parts…" Ruby offered.

"Nonsense! I love the marching, the neat uniforms, the feeling of being a part of something so much bigger than myself," Delores sat up straight and proud.

"That's true," Betty replied. "Reminds me of another old saying, 'You can't judge the size of the turnip by lookin' at the top."

The ladies clicked their glasses in the center of the table with a toast to all women in uniform. They chatted and passed the time all the way to Saint Louis, where Ruby would leave them, and Betty and Delores would board a train heading east. After tearful goodbyes and exchanging of addresses, the train chugged out of the station on the last leg of Betty's trip home.

Chapter Seventeen

A few days later, as the train pulled into the Charleston, West Virginia station, Betty peered out the window to see if she could see Nancy. She sent a telegram from the Cincinnati round house detailing the arrival schedule so Betty was reasonably sure her sister would be there. Delores bade her friend goodbye, knowing they would likely never see each other again. For a few years, Christmas cards would be exchanged, but as life moved forward, the cards would not follow.

Out on the wooden platform, Betty collected her bags and looked around. Suddenly, a head full of brown curls appeared, bouncing through the small crowd. Nancy rushed to wrap her arms around her favorite sister. She had brought Les along to the station. Holding his face in her hands, Betty saw the healed injury, the missing forearm and hand, and the happy tear in his remaining eye which looked directly at her. She held him closely for a few seconds before he pulled away and picked up one of the suitcases. Nancy grabbed the other one.

"I can get that!" Betty protested.

"Not in your condition, you don't! Oh, I'm so excited you are home!"

Nancy led them to her car. Along the several hour drive to Fayetteville they talked and talked. Betty learned Denver was stationed in England for some big operation, just as Tex thought he would be. She had three letters for Betty, one from the Army and two from Glenn. He had replied to her announcement of being pregnant with large capital letters, H O O R A H !!!! and confirmed he agreed with her plan of returning to West Virginia. He also mentioned the land in Dallas, and that his brother and nephew were going to help him start building a home. He hoped at least a few rooms would be ready before he brought her and the baby home to live there.

Being in Guam qualified him for an extended leave for reasons such as the delivery of a child. He would stay in Dallas for two to three months to work on the house and then travel to West Virginia for the baby's birth. Betty made a mental note to write him a long letter after she got settled.

When they drove into the New River valley and through Oak Hill, Betty was surprised how much it looked the same as it did when she left two years before. Nancy advised she should stay with their mother, as she was quite lonely and very excited about Betty's return. Nancy had moved in to keep Katherine company, and Nathan was on his way home from serving in the Army in England, so there was no room for Betty there.

Ethel held her daughter tightly for only a moment before commenting how thin she looked. Betty glanced at Nancy. Their mother was thinner than she ever had been, and had more gray hair, as well. The farm seemed smaller than Betty remembered— the cabin roofline lower and the tree line closer. She thought about all the wide open country she had seen and realized how much her knowledge of the world outside the farm in the Appalachians had expanded.

The two women fell into an easy routine, the hard work left to the McKinney kids who still came up the hill every day to help around the farm and have an afternoon snack with their grandmother and aunt. Ethel often made biscuits in the mornings and saved some for the children to eat with fresh milk and apple butter after the chores were done.

It was a happy time for Betty, seeing her nieces and nephews growing, observing Les excelling in his studies just as she had expected he would, and watching spring explode on the

154

mountain. She recalled the previous summer, time spent with Glenn, the hula dance, the heat of New Mexico.

As summer approached, Betty felt the changes occurring in her body and her abdomen began to protrude. Her sisters and sisters-in-law brought stacks of clean and neatly folded maternity clothes. She wore only a few of the dresses, the lighter weight fabric suited the warm, humid temperatures during the summer months. Nancy would drive out to the farm twice weekly to take Betty to Nathan's house for a proper bath and to visit with Mabel at the dime store. Those trips into town highlighted the seemingly endless days waiting for the baby to be born.

After the days became shorter and the children returned to school, Betty was quite miserable. Her back hurt, her feet swelled, and she felt overly warm both day and night. She received a telegram stating Glenn had arrived in Dallas and would be traveling to West Virginia with his nephew by car. They planned to arrive around September 15th.

Before leaving Carlsbad, Betty had several photographs printed of Glenn, herself, and her friends. Often she would take them out, gazing at the happy faces of Ruby and Tex, and Glenn's contemplative face in various stages of trying not to smile. Men in uniform were discouraged from smiling at all times, especially in photographs. She waited anxiously for his arrival.

During the morning of September 17th, a car with Texas license plates pulled into Fayetteville. Glenn noticed the dime store where he knew Betty had once worked. They parked in front and walked inside where Nancy happened to be purchasing new towels and wash cloths for Betty's upcoming delivery. When she saw the two men, she knew right away she was looking at a pair of Fields'. Mabel came out from around the counter to greet them. Nancy looked the taller man and saw the kindness in his face. She took initiative and approached him directly.

"You must be Glenn Fields," she said.

"Yes, ma'am, and this is my nephew, Jerry. And you must be a Nugen girl."

"This is Betty's sister, Nancy, and I'm Mabel. So glad to meet you, Betty has told us so much about you!"

"All good, I hope!" Glenn replied. "Where is she? Is she all right?"

"Of course, of course! You'll be wanting to get up there to the farm, I expect," Mabel offered.

"Yes, yes! Oh, I'm so glad to see you! Betty has been pretty miserable these past few weeks. I bet seeing you will perk her right up!" Nancy exclaimed.

"She's been ill?" Glenn asked.

"Oh, no." Mabel answered. "Just when you get close to having a baby, well, it isn't all that comfortable! Nancy, let's get these things put on your account and then we'll all go up to see Betty. Mr. Fields, I watched that girl grow up and she's a good one."

"Yes, ma'am, I know it. I was lucky to find a girl like her. And to think it was on an Air Corps base!"

The reunion was tearful and joyous. Glenn gave the proper respect to Ethel, and was overjoyed to see his bride. He touched her swollen belly gently, and instantly loved as he had never dreamed he could love. His wife and his child.

"When we married, I didn't have a proper ring for you. When I was in Dallas..." He knelt before her and presented a wedding ring set, with diamonds and in gold.

"Oh, my goodness. How beautiful! This must have been terribly expensive!" Betty accepted the rings and tried to put them on.

"All those months of pay had to go for something. I bought supplies to start the house and had enough left over to get this for you," he said, holding her hand.

"Fingers are too swollen. But I bet they'll fit better in a few weeks! Oh, thank you!" She placed her hands around his face and kissed him, right in front of everybody. When their lips touched, she knew she would be with this man for the rest of her life.

Betty knew the time was near. The baby was moving and the labor pains were beginning. On September 18, the doctor made the trip up the hill to see her. Unexpectedly, he was accompanied by the sheriff. After a quick examination of Betty and instructing her to sit down on a comfortable chair, he nodded to the other man. The sheriff shuffled his feet and glanced up at Ethel.

"Well, what is it?" she asked. She narrowed her eyes with suspicion. "This is about Paul, isn't it?"

"Yes, ma'am. It's been a long time since your son disappeared. Today a fisherman down at the river pulled up something that looked like it came from a car. When our man dove down into the water, he found a car. Paul's car."

Ethel straightened her back and nodded. She sighed once. "I knew he was dead. Now everyone knows it."

Betty sat back in shock. Glenn sat on one side of her and reached out to hold her hand. "Oh, no. I just knew he would appear one day saying, 'Here I am! I went to Canada and struck gold! Look, I'm rich, now' or some other silly thing. That would be our Paul."

Nancy sat on the bed. "Yes, I had hoped, too." She grasped Betty's other hand. They both fought back tears.

"I'm sorry to deliver this news. The death certificate will be prepared in a few days."

Ethel kept her back straight. "Thank you for bringing the news in person. At least it wasn't a telegram from the Army. Please, take a jar of our apple butter."

"This is never an easy thing to do. But, no thanks, ma'am, my wife can't eat apples."

Ethel and Mabel walked him out of the cabin.

The doctor took a closer look at Betty and said she was getting close, but he would come back the next day.

"Should we bring her to town? To the hospital? Glenn asked.

"No, no. This is a first child, there's plenty of time. Try not to be upset." The doctor gathered his things. "It is most unfortunate to receive such disturbing news so close to delivery."

Ethel pursed her lips. After the doctor left, she gathered the towels Nancy had brought and asked Glenn to draw a pot of water and put it on the stove. When Betty lay down to sleep beside her husband in the bedroom, Ethel sat in her rocking chair, watching and waiting.

Before dawn the next morning, Betty rose from the bed and felt the moisture from the embryonic sac gush from her body. She was frightened and yelled for her mother. Glenn jumped from the bed and made sure she was all right. He pulled on pants and a shirt as quickly as a soldier might be required to do.

"Ethel! Come quick!" He called out on the edge of panic.

Ethel came in the room with the towels. "You build up the fire in the stove to warm the water. Then outside with you!" She disappeared into the bedroom, shutting the door firmly behind her.

"Should I go get the doctor?" he called.

"No time for that. Send that nephew of yours down to Fanny's and bring her up here. Now, go!" Ethel yelled through the door.

After nervously setting the pot of water on the stove as instructed, Glenn stepped outside into the morning air to find Jerry. He had been sleeping on the side porch but heard all the noise in the house and rose to help. Glenn quickly told him to get in the car and bring the sister who lived at the bottom of the hill to the cabin. After the car left, he heard Betty's cries from the open window and cringed at each sound.

Unconsciously, he reached into a pocket to retrieve a pack of cigarettes. Then he remembered something for a few days before when they made a trip in to town. When he lit a cigarette, Betty sneezed so loudly people on the sidewalk stopped and stared. Grinning, he decided to stop the habit he had picked up in Guam. He didn't need the tobacco; it was just something to do. A burn barrel a few steps away accepted the package and he used some twigs, a book of matches, and the paper to set the fire. Nodding, he solemnly walked back to the porch.

Just after dawn, Glenn and Jerry stood on the porch feeling helpless and unneeded. Suddenly a different sound erupted from the window. The two men looked at each other and Glenn wrapped his arms around the nephew who was more like a brother. Ethel emerged from the cabin and motioned Glenn to come inside.

When he saw Betty holding the tiny baby, his heart melted into a large puddle. Sinking to his knees beside the old bed, he reached out to first touch Betty's beautiful face, wiped the tears from her eyes, and then gently felt the miniature hand of his child with the back of one finger. He rose and gave Betty a kiss on the forehead and turned to the women standing in the bedroom.

"It's a girl. A big, strong girl," Ethel advised.

"It's a little early to tell, but I think she has your eyes, Glenn Fields," Fanny teased.

"This is all, well, overwhelming. Thank you for helping her."

"She is family, that's what we do. I hope you remember, sir, wherever you take her, whatever you do, this will always be her home. She also was born in that very bed," Ethel said.

"Don't talk about me as if I wasn't in the room, please. Fanny, will you help me sit up?" Betty asked, struggling to her elbow.

"It might be too soon, take it easy, sister." Fanny hurried to help Betty to the side of the bed. The strong, farm woman had no problem propping up her younger sister.

"Now, then." Betty held the baby closely. "The way I see it, that old saying is true: home is where the heart is. And now, my heart can be in several places. Here, with Glenn in our home in

Texas. And with this baby wherever she goes and whatever she does. All those places will be home, but this farm and family are the roots," Betty said softly, as she leaned on Fanny.

"Very wise, my little mama. So you were born here and now this baby girl was born here, too. Yes, ma'am, we will make a home together, and our hearts will be wherever we are. And the heritage deep in this cabin and farm will indeed always make it our home."

The End

Epilogue

The graduation photo with the steer.

Betty, the WAC.

The Flight Jacket

The infamous hula outfit.

Glenn A. Fields, the man who won Betty's heart.

Glenn and Betty were married fifty-eight years and passed away within six months of each other. They are buried side-by-side in the DFW National Cemetery, as both had military status and were WWII veterans. They had two daughters, twelve years apart. Elaine, the author, and Carol, the baby born in West Virginia. Les McKinney went on to achieve a doctorate in mathematics and taught school on the college level. He and his Aunt Betty had a strong bond throughout both their lives. Betty kept in touch with her mother and most of her brothers, sisters, and sisters in law for many years. Paul Nugen was missing for seven years before a fisherman pulled up something from his car from the river.

Elaine wishes to acknowledge the contributions of many family members and friends during the creation of this book.

- Carol Fields Prater – the baby born in the cabin. She provided many memories and photos
- Joyce McKinney Dunn – with numerous photos and for her work with the Nugen family genealogy.
- Delores Thorp – the WAVE who shared much about life during WWII in the USA and her experiences.
- "WACs-the Women's Army Corps" by Vera Johnson – a wealth of information.
- Fred McKinney – for sharing the horrifying story of his brother's accident.
- Rick Nugen – for his memories of his father, Paul.
- Whoever scanned the newspapers of the time and Google for having them available to view. All the news stories came directly from those papers.

Special thanks to Pam Patterson for her friendship, support and fine line editing.

Elaine truly believes her parents are aware of this project, and she knows they are happy and proud of this book.

BLAZING STAR BOOKS

www.blazingstarbooks.com

Made in the USA
Columbia, SC
27 November 2020